THE DUNCANS ARE COMING

MICHAEL N. WILTON

1

FEAR NOTHING

'What a ridiculous sight I must look!' Lady Edith plucked fretfully at the webbing holding her down securely on the hospital bed. 'I don't know why I allowed myself to be talked into posing on this tractor equipment... or whatever it is they call it. What will all my friends think when they see me in the papers – specially that awful Muriel Fox-Cuddles? I shall be a laughing stock.'

'Traction, I believe is the term, my dear,' corrected her husband, his head buried in the Farmers and Landowners Gazette. 'Supposed to relieve tension, so they tell me.'

'Well, it's not relieving my tension.' Lady Edith tried to wriggle into a more comfortable position, without much success.

Draped over a more accommodating visitor's chair, her husband, Lord Beddington, was sunk in his own gloomy thoughts. 'Nor mine. I see land prices are going down again.'

'Land prices, that's all you ever think about, Henry. Oh, do stop reading that wretched paper, when you can see I'm suffering so. I feel like a turkey trussed up for Christmas.'

She sighed plaintively. 'It isn't as if I've got anything *wrong* with me. How can I possibly find the time to organise a full-blown charity festival at the Hall in less than three weeks to support St Mary's, if I've got to be stuck in this awful contraption half the afternoon – just for a publicity stunt. I've got enough to put up with already, getting all the committee members to agree on a programme, without all this. There'll be the rector wanting money for the church roof and that wretched Len Bartlett with his everlasting marina development scheme – I don't know how they ever let him loose on the Council – and what with Muriel bleating about fees for her Lavinia doing the PR, I doubt if we'll have any money left for the hospital. Why didn't *you* volunteer?'

Henry looked up, his expression mild. 'They tell me I don't project the right image, whatever that means, my dear. And as I seem to remember, you agreed to do it in the first place. Besides, who wants to see my ugly face in the local rag. Much rather have a good-looking gel, eh?' He went back to his paper again, searching hopefully for an answer to his problems. 'In any case, if I don't manage to sell some more of our land soon at the right price you won't be able to hold any more charity events at the Hall, because we'll be living in a crofter's hut in the Isle of Man, I shouldn't wonder. You've no idea what the estate's costing me – I blame the Government. All they care about are getting votes. No wonder people like ourselves are up the creek without a paddle.'

Lady Edith gave him a suspicious look and tried to smooth her hair. 'I'm sure it can't be as bad as you make out.' She returned to her personal grievance. 'It all seemed a good idea at the time as a way to launch the fund, seeing as they practically begged me to do it. But I didn't expect it to involve this kind of torture. You know, I'm sure Lavinia put this harness on the wrong way around. I should have had my head examined for letting her do it.'

To take her mind off his unfortunate remark, he looked

around the cosy little ward, seeking inspiration. Carefully averting his eyes from successive efforts to disguise the unmistakable architecture of a former Victorian workhouse, he argued loyally, 'After all, St Mary's is the only cottage hospital in this part for miles around. Where else will the people go if the blasted Ministry has its way and closes it down? It's got all the facilities you need, and some of the finest equipment available. Look at this traction bed, for example. Hrm, well perhaps not just now,' he added hastily. 'Anyway, it won't take long. Your PR girl, Lavinia 'what's- her- name', will be here any minute now with the photographer, before you can touch your toes.'

Seeing the look on her face, he hastily backtracked and tried to calm her down. 'Steady on, m'dear. All they want are one or two photos – just to show how marvellous the place is – and a few words from you to say what we all stand to lose if they pull it down.'

'I hope you're right,' snapped his wife. 'The sooner I get out of here the better, so I can get on with the things that matter. At least we were spared the horror of Roderick giving a hand.'

Lord Beddington coughed diplomatically. 'Funny you should mention that. I still remember the last time that, ahem, brother of yours was down here, organising that yachting race at West Creek.'

'Don't remind me,' fumed his wife. 'The idiot ended up sending them all aground at Wen Bank to crown it all, practically on our doorstep. and we had to pay to get them hauled off again. And he's supposed to be a General – just as well they didn't make him an Admiral. Good thing they posted him up to Scotland afterwards. No wonder they have such rotten weather up there – wouldn't mind betting he has something to do with that, as well.'

'Steady on, love. Anyone would think he was some sort of modern-day Genghis Khan. Not all the Duncans are like that, surely?'

3

But Lady Edith remained unconvinced. 'You didn't have to share the same nursery as I did, stuck up in that ghastly old family castle of ours in Scotland all those years – he was an absolute menace. Dumped all my favourite toys in the moat one Christmas just because he didn't get the toy tank he was after.' She quivered at the memory. 'And he was no better when he grew up. Swanked round the place as if he owned it and treated all the servants like serfs – thought they were all fellow travellers.'

'He's not still like that, surely?'

'You should have heard what happened when he dumped himself on our sister Vera last year, with his blasted lurcher widdling and what-notting all over the place. Never thought my sister knew that kind of language.' She snorted. 'It's bad enough having to have young William, that son of his, foisted on us instead. It was the only alternative I could think of when Roderick rang up the other week, offering to stick his oar in. Said he had a spot of leave coming up, and what about it? Wouldn't catch me giving him a second chance – he's an absolute menace, even if he is my brother. And I expect William's no better. Look what a mess he's made of his exams. It's probably some young woman he's running around with. That reminds me.' She stirred uneasily, as if expecting to see her nephew materialise from under the bed with a girl in tow. 'He is safe, isn't he? What have you done with him?'

'Don't worry.' Lord Beddington did his best to soothe her. 'Lavinia's looking after him; she's used to handling his sort. I expect he'll come in handy. We could do with some extra help, heaven knows. Anyway, I promised Roderick I'd teach him something about estate management while he's with us.' He pondered. 'Don't know how, mind you. I gather William's always babbling on about computer software and his latest conquests. That's what university does for you these days, I suppose. Trouble is, I don't know a thing about software, and

I'm too old to remember what the other kind of software was like.'

'Well I do wish she'd hurry – just like her mother, never on time when you want her.'

As if on cue, the swing doors at the end were flung back and a procession erupted into the ward, led by a distinctly ruffled Matron, waving her arms in agitation.

'Really, this is most irregular. We don't normally allow this sort of thing...'

Her protests were swept aside by a supremely confident young woman behind her who ushered in a slightly embarrassed photographer, helped by a fresh-faced young man who was ogling the girl so much he kept tripping over the suitcase of photographic equipment he was carrying.

'Ah, there you are, Lady Edith!' She rushed up to the bed, ignoring Lord Beddington. 'So good of you to volunteer.' Speaking loudly and clearly as if the patient was slipping away fast, she confided, 'I was just explaining to Matron all about the PR jollies we're planning. I'm Lavinia,' she explained to the ward at large, just in case anyone may have forgotten. 'I expect Mumsie's told you all about me. Splendid,' she carried on, not waiting for a reply. 'This is David, my photographer, and William – er... well anyway, he's sort of helping out.'

She threw them both a dazzling smile, and the sizzling impact made William gape wordlessly and drop the suitcase on the photographer's foot, turning the latter's greeting into a strangled grunt of agony.

'Good, that's got all that over.' Lavinia fixed them all with a confident air, like a hockey captain giving her team their last-minute instructions before going into battle. 'Mumsie's briefed me on the operation, and this is what we're going to do.' She caught sight of Lord Beddington. 'Excellent, I see we have a visitor. Now, what can we have you doing? I know, we'll pretend you're some sort of relative.'

'That's my husband!' Lady Edith found her voice at last. 'And how much longer am I supposed to be stuck on this wretched machine?'

Unabashed, Lavinia closed her eyes in creative meditation. 'Got it. We'll have you holding your wife's hand – you know, the dedicated bit. You can handle that? Splendid. Now then.' She eyed the patient, as if she'd have to do her best with the material she had been given. 'Lady Edith, what we want is a big look of tenderness for hubby who's been waiting all these weeks for you to get well and come home...'

'It's beginning to feel like that...' muttered Lord Beddington.

But Lavinia was already moving around to the other side of the bed, followed by the photographer who was developing a nervous twitch. She held up her hands to frame a picture and peered through, seeking inspiration.

'Great. This is it,' she enthused. 'We'll go for that big, big close-up of suffering. You've got to show those readers out there what wonderful things they are doing for you. It's only pretend, you understand, Lady Edith, you don't have to jump up and down like that until we start shooting,' she added in a jolly tone of voice.

'But I *am* suffering,' wailed Lady Edith. 'These straps are killing me.'

'Really, I must insist that Miss Serge, our physiotherapist, checks the equipment thoroughly before you start,' insisted Matron, appearing at her side, outraged at what was going on. 'Ah, here she is.' She signalled a masculine looking attendant hovering in the background who rushed forward in agitation.

'No-no, you must not use it – I left a notice. I am waiting for it to be repaired...'

'No time for that,' breezed Lavinia, kicking the notice under the bed. 'Now, quick as you can, David. This is how I see it. We do a quick shot from the end of this bed thing,' she whacked the cushion, causing Lady Edith to leap in anguish like a salmon at spawning time, 'then, another one from here...' She pushed William vigorously to one side to get a better view.

About to pass a tripod to the photographer, the unfortunate young man was catapulted towards the helpless patient, doing an excellent imitation of a rampaging Zulu warrior with an avenging spear as he did so. Even as he was hurtling towards her, he found himself making a rapid reassessment of his feelings for Lavinia, whose every move up to now he had been following devotedly. In desperation, William grabbed at the nearest support to hand – a ropelike cord hanging at the side of the bed.

'Do not press the button, I implore you!' shouted Miss Serge in a panic. 'I have not set the programme yet...' But the warning came too late.

In her far distant childhood, Lady Edith remembered in dazed recollection, she had been taken to the cinema by her nanny to watch a particularly bloodthirsty epic on the silent screen where the villain, laughing fiendishly, pulled a lever, leaving the victim at his mercy, about to be torn apart limb by limb, on a mediaeval contraption not unlike the one she was on. She knew instinctively what it must have felt like. But on this occasion she had no ice cream on hand from the usherette to comfort her. She only had the family motto of 'Fear nothing, hold fast' to sustain her. But it never really explained what one had to hold fast to, she thought inconsequently – which wasn't much good in her present situation. It was also of no help to her in what was to follow.

In a matter of seconds the harness at each end began to tighten, and the leather cushions she was lying on started to move apart, stretching her out like an elastic band – something the instruction manual had failed to mention.

Unaware of what was happening, the photographer was happily clicking away with his camera, lost in admiration at the acting performance put on by the patient.

Indeed, Lady Edith was screaming with such unrestrained abandon by this time that a group of patients in the other ward decided that they suddenly felt much better after all, and without enquiring further left there and then, some without bothering to dress.

'I say, it's not on,' Lord Beddington was complaining with growing conviction.

'Oh, don't bother,' Lady Edith managed feebly, getting up unsteadily and throwing off the straps. 'Just take me home while I'm still in one piece; get me out of here.'

But Lavinia was not finished. 'You were brilliant, quite brilliant. Now, I tell you what.' She pointed at his Lordship. 'Hubby's so overjoyed you've recovered, he reaches out in admiration – lots of macho here – and you fall in his arms. Fade out. Get the picture?'

She moved forward encouragingly, but Lady Edith was not convinced.

'Keep her away from me, Henry.' The terrified victim backed away so hastily that she half fell over a hospital trolly laden with bowls of soup and set it in motion. Lady Edith hung on as the trolly gained speed and shot past the traction bed, leaving a trail of destruction behind it, and crashed into a nurse polishing the floor. Demonstrating a beautiful arabesque movement, Lady Edith skidded the length of the ward and bounced back off the swing doors into the plump form of the anxious Matron and her muscular assistant.

When she came to, she reached up and touched a face. 'Oh, Henry, you've grown a moustache,' she said and came face to face with a furious Miss Serge. 'Ouch, my leg,' cried Lady Edith, and fell back.

But Miss Serge's pride and joy, her magnificent traction bed, was no longer in a fit state to be able to provide any more treatment. After a thorough examination of Lady Edith, the Matron announced, half fearful at the retribution that might fall on her as a result of the accident, and half excited at the prospect of treating such an eminent patient, 'I'm afraid you will be staying with us a little longer after all, your Ladyship. It looks as if you have broken an arm and a leg as well. Quite an interesting looking fracture too,' she added brightly.

'I say, what a splendid boost for our campaign,' burbled Lavinia. 'We'll get tremendous coverage now – I can just see the headlines.'

'You do realise what this means, Henry, don't you?' Lady Edith hissed, glaring at Lavinia. 'I shall not be able to organise the event – you will have to go in my place.'

'But I don't know the first thing about it...' began her husband, horrified.

'Don't worry.' The imperial spirit of Lady Edith was beginning to reassert itself once more. 'Come back this afternoon and I'll tell you what to do,' she hissed as she noticed Lavinia's ears beginning to flap. 'I'm not having a certain someone hijack this event. I'd like to see her try.'

Henry sighed. He knew that when his wife adopted that tone of voice, he had no option but to follow instructions, in the same dutiful way he took his medicine. 'I'll do my best, my dear.'

'Can I be of any help?' trilled Lavinia, rushing up, eager not to miss anything.

Lady Edith closed her eyes and counted silently to herself. 'No, thank you, Lavinia dear. I think you've done just about everything you possibly could at the moment. I was just telling Henry,' she thought rapidly for an excuse, 'how nice it would be to have some... of those gorgeous greengages that Jarvis grows so splendidly for us. We must make the most of them while they last. Would you do that, darling?'

Nonplussed, Henry blinked at his wife. 'Oh, ah, right. I'll see what I can do.' He got up hastily, recognising the royal inflection. It always seemed that Edith must have got that bit about 'honour and obey' mixed up somehow when they were married, because he was always the one who seemed to do all the jumping up and obeying bit.

'I'll come and give you a hand, Uncle,' said William quickly, sensing that Lavinia was about to ask him to stay and clear up. He didn't feel like getting involved with her in any further mayhem on the wards.

'You will?' said Henry, surprised at the unexpected offer. 'Oh, right-ho.' Then to escape from the inevitable question forming on Lavinia's lips, he excused himself hurriedly. 'Sorry I can't offer you a lift, my dear. Full up with equipment.'

'Bingo,' Lady Edith whispered with a wintry smile, as he bent to kiss his wife good-bye.

2

PRECIOUS CARGO

'I say, Uncle,' said William, as they got underway. 'Thanks awfully for the lift – it got me out of a nasty hole.'

'Had enough for one day?' asked Lord Beddington shrewdly.

'I don't mind *work*,' said William indignantly. 'It's that Lavinia – she's round the bend.'

Taken aback, Lord Beddington found himself changing into the wrong gear at the unexpected news. 'Sorry, my boy. Thought you were quite smitten, from the way you were gazing at her.'

William looked sheepish. 'Well, she is rather stunning, I give you that. But did you see what she did? If it wasn't for her barging into me like that, I wouldn't have gone anywhere near that blasted button. Aunt Edith must have thought I was bonkers.'

Lord Beddington coughed diplomatically. 'I don't expect she enjoyed the experience. On the other hand, I don't think she had time to work out how it happened.'

'I ask you, though, what a barmy thing to do. I was jolly glad to get away from her.'

'So you're not all that keen on Lavinia then?' His uncle wanted to make sure he had it straight from the horse's mouth.

'Keen on her?' laughed William bitterly, with all the wisdom and experience of a reformed twenty-two year old. 'I wouldn't be seen dead with her. She ought to be locked up.'

Lord Beddington beamed. His heart began to warm towards his young nephew. Perhaps he had the right stuff in him, after all.

'Look at all the trouble she's caused,' went on William indignantly. 'Now that Auntie's stuck in hospital, who's going to do all the organising for this event?'

'I'm afraid it looks as if I'm stuck with that now.'

'Exactly. And does Lavinia care? All she thinks about is her potty publicity. By the way, you can count me in for any help you want in that direction,' William offered. 'Not that I know much about that sort of thing – anything to do with committees and meetings bores me stiff.'

His uncle made sympathetic noises. 'You're not the only one. Never mind, there's always plenty more fish in the sea,' he added kindly.

'What kind of other fish are there, as a matter of interest?' William wanted to know.

'Come along to that meeting tomorrow and you'll see for yourself,' said his uncle, slightly amused. 'They tell me young Kate is quite a good looker, if she's there. That's Len Bartlett's daughter. Edith can't stand him, so I should watch your step where he's involved. Left wing, salt of the earth, but operates on a short fuse if you don't happen to agree with him, if you see what I mean.'

'Really. Thanks for the tip, Uncle.'

They drove along more cheerfully in companionable silence until they reached the imposing front gates of Beddington Hall. William admitted, 'I suppose I should have got used to it by now, but you've certainly got quite a pad here, Uncle – something to be proud of.'

'Nothing like it was at one time, my boy – pretty hopeless trying to keep it up these days.' Lord Beddington was lost in the past as he glanced sadly at the peeling paint on the gates and the crumbling brickwork either side, then mentally shook himself.

'Wait here. Hrm, best not to hurry, Jarvis will come and open the gates if we give him a bit of time.'

After a few minutes, William peered out. 'I can't see any sign of life in the lodge.'

There followed a few minutes of silence, then Lord Beddington tut-tutted, seeking inspiration. 'Must be his afternoon off. I know, I've got a key – we'll do it ourselves.' He got out, and after extracting an enormous key from his pocket opened the gates and they passed through. William was slightly mystified at why his uncle should have to carry such a large key around with him, but he kept such thoughts to himself. He was even more mystified after they reached the end of the drive and crossed the drawbridge over the moat to the massive front door, only to be told that the butler must be off duty as well. But by now he was getting used to his uncle, who followed up by fishing out an equally large duplicate key.

'Leave your bag there, the butler will see to it,' Lord Beddington told him with a forced air of heartiness. William did as he was directed, although he had the sneaking feeling his belongings would be there for some time. Meanwhile, his lordship wandered down the hall, humming to himself and calling out. 'Now, where the deuce is that gardener of mine. Jarvis?'

He put his head out of a window then went through an elaborate pantomime of searching the conservatory. 'Must be in the potting shed. I'll go and see.'

'I thought you said the lodge keeper was called Jarvis.'

'Oh, did I? I meant Jigger – rhymes with digger, d'you see?'

'It's probably his afternoon off as well,' joked William. His uncle gave a guilty start, and William suddenly felt sorry for him.

'Look, don't worry. There's no need to bother the gardener about a few greengages. Why don't you let me do it? All we need is a step ladder.'

'D'you know, I think that's probably a good idea,' agreed Lord Beddington with relief. 'Let's go and see.'

The only ladder they could find in the potting shed looked as if it was last used in the Crimean war. It was wedged between a rusty hose and what appeared to be an arsenal of muskets and cannon balls. The woodwork was full of woodworm, and several of the rungs were either missing or broken.

'Absolutely ideal,' boomed Lord Beddington.

William studied it dubiously. 'Okay, if you say so, Uncle. Now, tell me where this greengage tree can be found.'

'I'll do better than that, my boy,' said his Lordship gratefully. 'Follow me, I know exactly where it is.' And with that, he led the way to the fruit tree which turned out to be only a dozen yards away, but it took half an hour of false starts and hesitations before they reached it via a very circuitous trail.

'Mind if I sit down, my boy? I don't seem quite as spry as I used to,' Lord Beddington panted.

'No, go ahead, Uncle. Just tell me which ones you want.' He climbed rather gingerly up the rickety ladder and was just reaching out for a particularly juicy greengage when he gave a shout of recognition.

'What is it, my boy. Are you all right?'

William waved reassuringly to the anxious face below. 'I'm fine. Just discovered where we are. There's the Hall over there, isn't it?'

'Good lad,' encouraged Lord Beddington from the comfort of the grass bank. 'I think you and I make a jolly good team.'

Taking a look around from his lofty perch, William was amazed at the view. 'Wow, the estate stretches for miles, right up to the coast. You've even got your own bay, by the looks of it.'

'Yes, that's Wen Bank, they call it – your father knows all about that.'

'Oh, yes, he did mention something about a regatta ending up there,' admitted William ruefully. Changing the subject, he said, 'It must cost a mint to run – how do you manage to look after it all?'

'I sometimes wonder that myself, my boy,' agreed Lord Beddington in a burst of candour. 'How I'm supposed to run this wretched place and organise a blasted festival at the same time is beyond me.'

'I know what you want.' William jumped down in a state of excitement. 'You want a computer – I can hire one from the nearest town and work out the whole thing for you. Wouldn't cost you much.'

At the mention of money Lord Beddington was on his feet in a panic. 'This needs thinking about. Look, let me pick some of those greengages, I insist. It's my turn. I'll have a go with this rake.'

Reluctant to let go of his favourite topic, William ploughed on. 'But Uncle, don't you realise...'

'I realise that if I don't get those greengages back to Lady Edith this afternoon, I shall be in the mire. Now out of the way, William my boy, I'm taller than you and I can see some beauties at the top.'

'Do you think you ought to, Uncle? It's a long way up and a bit shaky going, for your... all that way up,' he amended hastily.

'Nonsense, my boy. I was picking greengages before you were born. You watch me.'

William held the ladder grudgingly and followed his uncle's progress with mounting unease. At last he could not stay silent any longer. 'We've got plenty now, Uncle. Why don't you come down?'

'Nearly finished, must get that whopper over there – it's the best of the bunch…'

Suddenly, William let out a whoop which startled Lord Beddington so much he lost his footing for a moment and dropped the rake, grabbing helplessly at the nearest branch.

Unaware of his predicament, William's face lit up with enthusiasm.

'I've just had another brilliant idea, Uncle. Why don't you let me get a laptop and feed in all the information about the estate? That way, you'll know exactly where all the money goes – and you can plan ahead. It's as easy as falling off a log!'

Lord Beddington knew nothing about computers – the thought of laptops reminded him of his youthful scuffles with his first secretary – but the very idea of contemplating such a step froze the blood in his veins, despite the hot afternoon sun. If falling off a log was considered easy, he quickly demonstrated that falling off a tree was even easier if you went about it the right way. His foot slipped again and went through several broken rungs, then he gathered speed and slithered down the rest of the way, ending up on the ground with half the ladder wrapped around his head.

'Stay there,' said William anxiously, propping him up against the tree, 'I'll get some help.'

'Don't worry,' groaned his uncle. 'I don't think I'll be going anywhere very far.'

Remembering the direction back to the house from the top of the tree, William was able to reach the phone in double quick time and rang the emergency service.

As the stretcher team struggled through the undergrowth to the orchard, Lord Beddington raised a hand in greeting.

'Ah, there you are, Jarvis.' He motioned to the ladder. 'Can you get this damned thing off?'

Jarvis inclined his head respectfully. 'I am sorry I was not here to prevent this unfortunate occurrence, m'lord. I was doing my St John's Ambulance turn.' His eyes gleamed at the sight of the ladder. 'I've been looking everywhere for that, m'lord.'

'Well, you can have it with my blessing. It seems to have become quite attached to me.'

His lodge keeper-cum-butler-cum-gardener applied his hand to the task with the help of William and the ambulance man. They all tugged and strained, then reluctantly gave up.

'It appears to be somewhat loath to leave you, m'lord. I fear they will have to deal with it at the hospital.'

'Well, take some tools along, just in case.'

'Yes, m'lord.'

'Oh, and William...'

'Yes, Uncle?' William leaned over, expecting some momentous news.

'Better pick up those greengages, otherwise I shall never hear the last of it.'

'Oh, thank goodness you've arrived, Doctor Medway!' The plump matron practically dragged him into the entrance. 'We've just heard that his Lordship is on his way. He'll be here any minute.'

The worthy doctor raised his eyebrows. 'He's a bit late. Haven't they taken those photographs yet?'

'You don't understand.'

'All right, give me a chance to get my breath back, I've just been to a road-side emergency and I need a bit of a clean-up.'

'You haven't got time for that.' She yanked at his arm impatiently, and he found himself being propelled, protesting, into the ward.

'Hi, mind my arm, I think I've sprained a muscle or

something at that accident. Any chance of a session on that traction machine of yours? It might be just what I need.'

Matron laughed hysterically. 'That's what her Ladyship thought, and look what happened to her!'

Doctor Medway surveyed the scene blankly. The traction bed had a large sign that read, 'Do not use - under repairs', and Lady Edith was the centre of attention, with an arm and a leg swathed in bandages and raised on pulleys. Just then another patient was wheeled by with remnants of a ladder around his head. Looking closer, the doctor recognised him and laughed uncertainly.

'Really. Isn't this carrying publicity a bit too far?'

Unable to get anything out of a distraught Matron, Dr Medway turned to William for an explanation.

'It's no laughing matter, Doctor. Aunt Edith's had an accident and broke an arm and a leg, and Uncle Henry's fallen down a ladder and done the same thing.'

'Has anyone seen to his Lordship?'

'Yes,' said William distractedly, 'they've just called for a carpenter.'

'But this is terrible,' gasped Dr Medway. 'What are we going to do?'

'I know,' William agreed feverishly. 'It means they'll be out of action for at least a month.'

'Dreadful, simply dreadful.' The doctor looked around wildly.

William pressed his arm in sympathy. 'It could be worse, I suppose.'

'But you don't understand,' moaned the doctor. 'Now this has happened, who's going to be responsible for organising the festival? We've got a meeting tomorrow!'

Nobody answered his cry from the heart, and as Lord Beddington was being eased onto a bed, Lady Edith caught sight of him and called out anxiously, 'Is that Henry? You haven't forgotten my greengages, have you?'

William went pale on hearing the voice and pressing his precious cargo of fruit in the hands of the surprised doctor, hurriedly left with a muttered excuse.

3

A MATTER OF CHOICE

As William carefully picked his way down the staircase the next morning, drawn by a tantalising smell of coffee and looking like an elderly spider with a wooden leg, he was vaguely aware of two things. One, he had a splitting headache, and two, he could have sworn he was being followed by a detachment of the Household Cavalry. He peered behind with some trepidation and was relieved to find the staircase empty, although to his untrained eye it seemed to be tilting to one side. Stooping, he removed his slippers which reduced the noise fractionally, and clutching the top of his head he tottered down the last few steps and sniffed his way to the breakfast room.

It did not make him feel any better when he got there to see Jarvis sedately putting out a variety of heated silver dishes on the sideboard, filling the room with a rich aroma of cooking smells.

'Good morning, sir.' Jarvis stepped forward courteously. William suddenly noticed he was dressed impeccably as a butler down as far as his waist, but below that he was wearing a pair of old gardening trousers. Hurriedly averting his gaze,

William was startled to hear a voice so close behind him it made him jump.

'No, thank you, Jarvis.' He shuddered. 'Just black coffee.'

'Certainly, sir.' Jarvis took one look at him and disappeared from view like a genie returning to its lamp. To William's relief he reappeared in a flash, holding a steaming percolator which he placed on the table. Then, magically, he produced a small glass containing a peculiar looking dark brown mixture which he held out with the same air of reassurance that William's nanny used to employ. Trustingly, William reached out blindly and gulped it down. After the first shock waves had passed, the sound of hammering began to recede to a respectful distance and William felt strangely comforted.

Jarvis awaited his verdict.

Running his tongue around his mouth experimentally, William pondered for a while like an expert at a wine tasting ceremony and delivered his judgement. 'It tastes like rotting vegetables with a hint of Zambesi mud thrown in.'

Nodding as if satisfied, Jarvis picked up the percolator.

'His Lordship used to put it a little more colourfully. Would you care for some coffee now, sir?'

William reached out with a shaking hand and swallowed gratefully. 'Another two gallons of that, Jarvis, and I'll begin to feel nearly human.' Then, feeling an explanation was due, he confessed, 'I expect you heard what happened at the hospital yesterday? I tell you, I felt so browned off after that fiasco, I called in at the pub on the way back and had a few drinks to stave off the nightmares.'

'So I understand, sir.' Jarvis stepped forward and refilled the cup with a careful eye. 'Have you heard the latest news about his Lordship and Lady Edith?'

William clutched his cup. 'Why, has anything else happened?'

'I merely asked because the next meeting regarding the

festival arrangements is being held at 10 o'clock this morning in the West Wing, and Dr Medway, who is attending, may hopefully have some further information on the subject.'

'I say, I'd better get there and find out.' William looked up quickly, and found to his surprise his head was still in one piece. 'What's the time now?'

'I believe it is just after half past ten, sir. Can I be of any further assistance?'

'Yes, you can show me where the West Wing is,' said William, jumping to his feet guiltily.

'Certainly. If you will allow me, sir?' He whipped out a handkerchief and tucked it into William's top pocket with a flourish. 'We mustn't appear undressed, must we?'

'Right, that reminds me...'

'Yes, sir?'

William eyed the butler's clothes and the question trembled on his lips.

'Er, never mind. Let's go and see what the doc has to say, but not too quickly,' he cautioned.

Meanwhile, in the west wing, the doctor's usual calm bedside manner had deserted him and for once he was at a loss for words. His eyes were almost popping out of his head as he stared, speechless, at the photographs Lavinia was passing him with an air of modest triumph.

'...and that's the one where Lady Edith tries to leap out of the traction bed, and here she is hitting the trolly... and this one is brilliant. Just look at Lord Beddington with that silly old ladder around his head.'

Doctor Medway found his voice at last. 'Thank heavens you've shown them to me first. I'll put these away where nobody'll see them.'

Lavinia smiled indulgently. 'Don't worry, Medders, we've

got plenty more copies.' She plonked a pile of newspapers in front of him.

'There you are, we had enough to get them in all the papers.'

The doctor clutched his head. 'Good grief! Look at that!'

'Yes, we thought that one was pretty good, didn't we, Mumsie?' She thumbed through the papers and chortled. 'What about this one where they're sliding along the floor. Priceless!'

'Oh, no,' said her mother, purring, 'I still think the one where she is hitting the ceiling in the traction bed is the best. So like dear Edith, don't you think? And I *do* like that caption! "New shock campaign to save local hospital." Oh, and they've given a quote to you, darling. How nice.'

'Where, oh where?' said Lavinia, jumping up and down.

'Just after the bit where they say, "The latest campaign to help bring a halt to the Government's economy drive on hospital shut-downs got off to a sizzling start yesterday when Lady Beddington put a new meaning into patient care, in a scorching performance that goes to show there is nothing she will not do to save the threatened closure of our local cottage hospital." Here we are, I'll read it. "In an exclusive interview, attractive twenty-three year old Lavinia Fox Cuddles, who is coordinating the campaign, said, "Lord and Lady Beddington have gone out of their way to show what kind of treatment everyone can expect to get from St Mary's. I think we have done our bit to prove this."'

She broke off. 'Why, doctor, are you all right? Lavinia, help me get him up. He seems to have fainted.'

'They say a good shock helps to bring them round.'

Dubiously. 'I think he's already had that, dear. Stop shaking him and think of something nice to tell him.'

'Medders,' whispered Lavinia dutifully. 'It was all a joke.'

'Wha-at, what?' Dr Medway raised his head hopefully. 'Tell me it isn't true.'

'It isn't true – but I'm lying,' obliged Lavinia. 'Don't you see, Medders, what marvellous publicity it all is? Everyone is talking about our campaign.'

'They certainly are,' agreed the doctor moodily. 'What will Lord and Lady Beddington say when they see this?'

'Never mind that.' Mrs Muriel Fox Cuddles pointed at the paper with shining eyes. 'Now we'll *have* to find someone else to carry on.'

Lavinia read the sentence aloud. "The condition of both Lord and Lady Beddington, who are reported to have sustained broken arms and legs during this energetic PR exercise, raises the intriguing question of who will take over the reins of organising the appeal in the short time left available. It is rumoured that anyone interested will be strongly advised to acquire some knowledge of first aid."

'Now I wonder what we are going to do about finding a new organiser at this stage?' Muriel Fox Cuddles looked meaningly at her daughter who was searching for some more quotes about herself in the other papers.

'Mmm?' Lavinia caught on at last. 'Mumsie, why don't you do it. You'd be ideal!'

'Do you really think so?' Her mother gave the impression of being suitably surprised. 'Of course, I have been complimented on organising my musical soirees at the vicarage...'

'That's a great help,' commented the doctor drily, privately aghast at what Lady Edith would think of such a proposal.

'...and I have been chief opposition leader on the Council for over six years,' she added sharply. 'With Lavinia handling the PR side I should get voted on as leader now, as well as taking over as organiser of this hospital do. We should be able to wrap it up between us quite nicely.'

'What's that you're going to wrap up, fish and chips?'

interrupted a familiar voice belonging to their old enemy on the Council as he entered the room breezily. 'Put me down for a large portion. Didn't have time for breakfast with all the meetings I've got lined up. Good thing Kate's picking me up, otherwise I'll never make it.'

'I thought it wouldn't be long before you turned up and lowered the tone of the meeting, Len Bartlett,' she sniffed.

'Now don't say that. I was just about to compliment Lavinia on her press coverage.'

'Oh? I'm glad someone has something nice to say.' She eyed him suspiciously.

'Yes, best bit of publicity for the party I've seen all year. Up the working classes. Not that I have anything against Lady Beddington personally, mind. But with her out of the running as Council Chairman, we need to pick someone else to take over that little job as well – and I don't think we need to look very far, do we?' He puffed his chest out expectantly.

'Really! Everyone was just saying how well I would fit the position.' She preened herself. 'Besides, you're always saying you can't find time to do anything else with all your meetings.'

Len Bartlett bridled. 'I can organise anything a darn sight better than you can ever do. And you're supposed to be leader of the Council's so-called opposition. Talk about a wet nanny. You couldn't even organise a sailor's farewell. Now as I see it, we ought to broaden the appeal to take in my idea for a new marina. Just by chance I happen to have the plans with me...'

Doctor Medway broke in hastily, seeing Muriel Fox Cuddles get up furiously. 'I think it would be better if we could find a more national figure. I know, what about our MP?'

'Oswald Plunk?' questioned Muriel, unconvinced. 'He's far too busy setting up committees to encourage tourism to worry about our little local events, I'm afraid.'

'You mean he's too scared to go against his precious Government hospital closures,' taunted her visitor.

'How dare you.' Mrs Muriel Fox Cuddles was on her feet. 'At least he's doing something to bring money in, not pottering around with some crack-pot bucket and spades scheme that will ruin our lovely port.'

'Bucket and spades scheme?' spluttered the Len Bartlett, red-faced. 'I've a good mind to...'

'...ask someone else who could carry on the family tradition?' interrupted the doctor desperately. 'Ah, there you are, William.' He wiped his forehead in relief. 'Come in, my boy. You know Lavinia, but I don't think you know her mother, Mrs Muriel Fox Cuddles, who leads the Opposition party on our Council... and Mr Bartlett, also a member, who, um, looks after our local port affairs. This is William ah... Lord Beddington's nephew,' he introduced hurriedly.

'How d'you do.' Len Bartlett stretched out a hand brusquely. 'Don't say you're putting yourself forward for the job?'

William looked surprised. 'Me?' He was about to go on when a very attractive redhead came in and quietly sat down next to Len Bartlett. At the sight of her, William's jaw sagged in slow motion, his legs buckled under him and he sat down suddenly, an inane grin spreading over his face.

Noticing everyone looking at him, he smiled weakly, unable to take his eyes off the newcomer.

'I'm, er, just here for a couple of weeks till next term to learn something about estate management. At least, I was...' He turned guiltily to the doctor. 'Have we heard how they are?'

The doctor looked at his watch. 'No, I hope to have some news later on this morning. That reminds me I must be off for my hospital rounds soon.'

A speculative expression came into Mrs Muriel Fox Cuddles' eyes. Baulked at the possibility of losing out on the coveted hospital appeal job herself, an idea for scoring off Lady Edith suddenly occurred to her and she almost hugged herself at the uproar it would cause. 'I've just had a thought. Why don't we ask your father, General Duncan, if he can do it? Take over running the festival, I mean.'

William blinked at her in surprise. 'I believe he did offer to help, but...'

Seizing the suggestion with overwhelming relief, like a daisy being revived in a shower after a long drought, the doctor gulped. 'What a splendid idea. I didn't know your father was General Duncan. Does he know this part of the world?'

'Oh, extremely well,' Mrs Muriel Fox Cuddles lied smoothly. 'Why, he was the one who organised that regatta for us. They all know him round here. His name's a household word.'

'Duncan?' echoed the Len Bartlett thoughtfully. 'I seem to have heard that name somewhere before...'

The doctor's face brightened. 'I've only been here a few months so I wouldn't know. I'd better let Lady Edith know. She will be pleased.'

'Oh, I wouldn't do that until I've had a word with Dad,' said William, paling at the thought.

'And I'll help you brief him on the background,' added Lavinia brightly, anxious not to be left out. Her mother nodded approvingly.

Seeing himself being edged out, Len Bartlett was quick to take advantage of the goofy look William was bestowing upon his daughter.

'Tell you what. Seeing as how I'll be tied up in meetings over the next few weeks anyway, why don't I get Kate here to liaise with you on this, so I can keep posted about what's going on?' Before anyone could protest, he beamed, and said, 'You haven't met my daughter, have you? Kate, this is William Duncan, Lord Beddington's nephew.'

'How d'you do,' Kate murmured politely in a soft voice that sounded to William like a harp playing on a distant shore, making him gape even more.

'Rather...'

'Excellent. I'll leave you two to get together and sort something out. Come along my dear, otherwise I'll miss my next meeting.'

William watched with open mouth as Kate rose and followed her father with relief. Lavinia and her mother glanced at each other meaningly.

'Now what about asking your father?' suggested Lavinia, advancing purposely on William.

A few minutes later William was ringing up his father, only to find that the General would not be back until later that evening.

'Supper,' murmured Muriel Fox Cuddles in passing.

'I know, William,' exclaimed Lavinia, as if struck by a bright thought.' Why don't we grab a bite to eat somewhere. Then you can ring up your father later on and get it all zipped up.'

Backing away nervously, William stalled. 'Can't it wait till tomorrow? Dad sometimes gets back awfully late. In fact, he's rarely in...'

Lavinia pouted and turned on the charm. 'Don't say you're losing interest? Anyone would think you wanted to organise it all by yourself.'

Feeling trapped, William gave in. 'All right, but not anywhere too public,' he said, thinking it might get back to Kate. 'Why don't I get Jarvis to knock us up something here, in the dining room?'

Lavinia's eyes widened. 'Oh William, how romantic. D'you mean just the two of us?'

'Just in case we have to hang around on the phone, waiting for Dad to get back,' stuttered William, turning red.

'Naughty, naughty,' whispered Lavinia. 'I'll be there. I just *love* playing waiting games. Shall we say eight o'clock?'

.   .   .

Like a well-trained daughter she phoned her mother as soon as she got back to her flat, to get her approval and to marshall her tactics like any self-respecting PR partner before meeting a prospective client.

'You've done very well,' was the verdict. Then came the electrifying news that sent a tingle through her daughter. 'Listen, darling, I've been doing some checking up on that Duncan family, and guess what?'

'What?' said Lavinia, her curiosity aroused.

'That General Duncan's aunt owns a castle up in Scotland and he stands to collect a packet when she kicks the bucket. Someone told me she's worth over a million!'

'Pounds or dollars?'

Her mother came back quicker than a calculator. 'Pounds, of course, silly.' She paused to meditate. 'Such a nice young man, I thought – that is as long as you're not still struck on that American airman you were going out with – what was his name, Chuck or someone?'

But Lavinia was not listening. She was already one step ahead of her mother, sorting out her bridesmaids and deciding on a suitable holiday home in the south of France. In the middle of it all, a happy thought struck her. 'We'll be able to charge a whacking great fee for organising the festival now.'

There was a reverent sigh down the phone. 'Pull this one off, darling, and we'll be able to open up a new PR company in Scotland. Just think of all those chargeable overheads.'

Her daughter was lost for a moment in a swirl of rosy dreams. Then she looked at her watch and came to earth with a bump. 'Golly, look at the time. I must fly. And I haven't got a thing to wear.'

'What about that rather short flimsy outfit you wore last summer?'

'But Mumsie, I could hardly get into it then...'

Her mother's voice was full of innocence. 'I'm sure you could if you tried. Bye, best of luck.'

Lavinia put the phone down thoughtfully. She knew a good thing when she saw one, and this had a green light flashing for her all the way. With a happy smile of anticipation, she reached out for her best silk stockings.

4

JARVIS DISAPPROVES

Anxious not to give Lavinia any reason to think he was trying to create a favourable impression, William decided to keep the supper date as casual as possible. He went through his clothes, picking out the most disreputable items he could find that would have him thrown out of even the seediest coffee bar in Soho. As a result, he found himself dressed in the threadbare jeans and check shirt he normally wore at the university. Despite the looks of disapproval from Jarvis as he was laying out the table, William was sure that his guest would conclude that he was totally uninterested in her.

He was therefore completely unprepared for the glamorous vision that floated into the Hall just before eight, attired in a breath-taking outfit.

'Lavinia?' he said uncertainly, trying to recognise the jolly hockey stick leader behind the super model swaying in front of him.

A slender hand moved out and brushed him on the chest and immediately the spell was broken. It was the same beefy impact he remembered that sent him flying in the direction of the traction bed the previous afternoon.

'Oh, William,' she simpered, 'if I'd known it would be so cosy, I would have worn something different. I feel almost overdressed.'

William blinked at the wispy garment that barely covered her bare essentials. It clung to her so tightly, he thought it was only a matter of time before something ghastly happened. He was conscious of further looks of disapproval from Jarvis who was hovering in the background.

'Shall I start serving now, sir?'

'Yes, why not,' he said hastily. 'Would you like to sit here, Lavinia? An extra cushion, perhaps,' he added as he watched her lower herself gingerly on the chair and shut his eyes, waiting for the inevitable rending sound. When he opened them again he saw she had miraculously managed the feat, causing her hem line to rise alarmingly, exposing an inviting expanse of thigh. And above her waist, her twin peaks jutted out so dangerously it reminded him irresistibly of scaling the Himalayan heights.

'I'm fine,' Lavinia protested, leaning forward as if to prove it.

'I think I'll just have another go at ringing up Dad, while we're waiting,' his said, voice almost cut off through lack of oxygen.

'Don't be too long,' she cooed.

When he returned, it was with a listless expression that told its own story. 'No luck, not back yet.'

'Never mind.' She patted his hand again and nearly scattered his place setting. 'You can tell me all about yourself.' But it was quite obvious from her questions where her real interest lay. 'Do tell me, is it true your family live in a real castle? And have you got oodles of mon... servants?' she corrected herself in time. She leaned even closer to give him full value.

William found himself babbling away. Yes, there was a castle but not too many servants. He didn't know how many.

Yes, it was quite a fair size, about 400 acres. And yes, his father did have a wealthy aunt who was getting on a bit. About eighty-six, he thought.

Had he been looking at her while was answering he would have seen her eyes flashing like a cash register as the Brownie points were mounting up in his favour.

After the last dish had been cleared away, Lavinia stretched out contentedly.

'That was super. If I eat any more, I'll burst out all over.'

Half afraid it might happen at any moment, William made his excuses and fled to the phone. This time there was a delay and when he came back he was in a happier frame of mind.

'He's back.' Then in answer to her unspoken question. 'It's no good, he won't do it. Absolutely refuses.'

'But why?' Lavinia was aghast. 'What did he say?'

'He was furious. Apparently, he suggested it the other day and Uncle turned him down flat. Made him hopping mad. Said something about them being a stuffy lot of conservatives and the place was full of bureaucrats and they deserved all that was coming to them when the time came.'

'What is he, some kind of evangelist?' Lavinia sounded worried.

'No, nothing like that,' said William regretfully, searching for some excuse to put her off. He cleared his throat. 'I suppose some people would regard him as an extreme type. Definitely not the sort of person to organise things socially, if you know what I mean. He's not exactly a rabid nationalist, but he's very anti-red, he'd do anything if he saw a chance to score off them. Damn lot want stringing up, I've often heard him say.'

'Would he now?' said Lavinia softly. 'Let me talk to him, William. I think I might be able to change his mind.'

Relieved at the chance of escaping another close encounter, William jumped back and made tracks for the phone again, half intrigued to know what powers of persuasion she would use.

Giving William a conspiratorial wink, Lavinia spoke earnestly into the mouthpiece.

'Am I really speaking to *the* General Duncan? I am? This is Lavinia Fox Cuddles. I'm co-ordinating the PR side of this operation. Well now, I don't know whether William had the chance to tell you *all* the facts? It's not just a question of organising a festival – anyone could do that. It's far more serious. If I tell you that *national security* comes into it, that would be a different matter, wouldn't it? I see we're talking the same language, General.' She lowered her voice. 'I was talking to Gerald the other day and he was in a terrible state about it. Yes, that's right, the Lord Lieutenant, d'you know him? No, I'm so glad.' She went on smoothly, 'What I meant was, I'm so glad I can tell you what's worrying him. He was saying it's only a matter of time before the Reds take over here. Yes...the local Council's absolutely *riddled* with them. And when we heard there was a chance we might get you to look after the festival so you could keep an eye on things, we were absolutely *delighted*. No, there's been nothing in the press. It's all hush-hush, you understand. Can we count on your support? You want to speak to William? Yes, I'll put him on...' She held out the phone to William and crossed her fingers.

'Dad? Yes, it's me, William. Why didn't I tell you? Well, er...' He looked at Lavinia helplessly. She nodded vigorously. 'Yes, I understand there is a rather left-wing element on the Council. No, I've never met the Lord Lieutenant. You will? Right, I'll tell Jarvis to get a room ready. How many?'

William put the phone down with a barely concealed groan. 'He's coming the day after tomorrow and he's bringing half his staff with him.'

Grabbing him in her arms, Lavinia waltzed him around the room. 'Super! Great! What did I tell you?'

Wincing from the grip, William freed himself. 'What was all that about a revolution? You didn't tell me you knew the Lord Lieutenant.'

'Didn't I?' Lavinia said carelessly. 'You'd be surprised who I get to know, doing PR. You must admit it sounded good.'

William started getting alarmed. 'That's not the point. Was it all true? If Dad finds out you've been stringing him along, there'll be all hell to pay. And I know who'll be blamed.'

'Now don't worry. Tell you what.' She linked her arm in his. 'Why don't you give me a quick guided tour and then I must be off.'

Seeing him waver, she wheedled, 'It will have to be a quick one. I've never been to the Hall before. Come on, if we've got to get this show on the road right away, I have to know the layout so I can work out where we're going to hold the functions. Right?'

His face cleared. 'Yes, of course. Well, Jarvis is the best person to show you around. I'll call him.'

Before he could do so, she swung him around in the opposite direction with surprising ease and, grabbing a bottle of wine in passing, headed for the stairs.

'No time for that. Tell you what, we'll start at the top, then it'll be quicker coming down.'

It wasn't until they reached the top landing that William thought to ask about the wine.

'A celebration,' Lavinia said mysteriously. Then to distract him, she darted ahead, peering into the nearest room. 'Is this where you hang out? What a ducky little bedroom, just right. Now, where're the glasses? These'll do,' she giggled, emptying some toothbrushes out of a couple of plastic cups on a shelf over the hand basin. 'Oh, get me a bottle opener, William, will you?'

'Don't think there is one...' began William, looking nonetheless in the hope of getting rid of her. As soon as he disappeared into the bathroom, Lavinia opened her sling bag and slipped a tablet into one of the cups.

'Not to worry!' she cried heartily, smashing the neck of the bottle against the basin and pouring out the wine in one swift movement. 'We don't need an opener after all. I learned this in the Girl Guides.'

William took the proffered cup dubiously, while Lavinia urged him on.

'Drink up. Here's to the beginning of a new and special stage in our relationship.'

Lavinia drank hers in a quick practiced gulp and put the cup down, ready for what was to follow.

'Are you sure this is all right...?' started William. Then as he dropped the cup and started yawning, she swivelled him round so that he fell straight back across the bed in one go.

'Well, that's the first bit. Now, let's see how easy the rest of it goes. Early to bed, early to rise. This is where we give William a hell of a surprise.' And she bent down and started untying his shoe laces.

When he came to the next morning with a splitting head, William could have sworn it was the night before last he had that bender at the pub. Then as his memory came flooding back and he discovered he only had his pants on, his first thought was. *Hell, what am I doing practically starkers?* As a dreadful suspicion grew, he cautiously felt sideways and encountered warm flesh.

He rolled over and saw soft hair spread out over the pillow and for a wild fleeting moment he thought longingly of Kate. Propping himself up on one elbow, he peered over her shoulder and saw the serene and smiling face he was beginning to know so well.

'Oh, my God,' he groaned. He took a second look to make

sure and saw much more besides. Rounded things and curves and little else. Just as he was summoning up enough courage to creep out of bed and make a dash for it, Lavinia opened her eyes and smiled up at him.

'Hello, lover boy.'

'Lover boy?' William stared at her, aghast. 'What do you mean, I never touched you. I'd have known...'

Showing just the right amount of modesty mingled with adoration, Lavinia spoke feelingly. 'Oh, William, you were wonderful. I never knew it would be so heavenly.'

'But-but...' he stammered. 'I didn't. You know I didn't. It's not true. Tell me it's not true!'

For a moment, Lavinia was tempted to agree, just as she had with the doctor, then she steeled herself. 'It's true, all right. You don't know your own strength, you naughty boy.'

In desperation, William reached out, pleading, 'Lavinia, be reasonable, just this once.'

'That's what you said last night,' echoed Lavinia dreamily. 'And look what that led to.' Then as he began to advance, she slipped out of bed smartly. 'That's enough, more than enough, darling. I shall be worn out at this rate. You'll just have to be patient and wait until we're married.'

'Married?' William began to feel he was in a nightmare and pinched himself. 'Ouch.'

'Ouch, indeed, you naughty boy.' She kissed him on the top of the head and skipped to the phone. 'Just wait till I tell Mother!'

'No, don't! Let's talk this over.'

But being a good PR girl, Lavinia wanted to spread the news right away and couldn't keep it to herself any longer. 'Mumsie, guess what! William and I are engaged. Yes, isn't it thrilling? It was all so sudden, I can't believe it's happening, isn't that right, William darling?'

He nodded dumbly.

'Can he speak to you? William, Mumsie wants to say hello. She's so pleased.'

William mumbled wordlessly. The bright morning light was suddenly banished from sight, and all he could feel was a black blanket of despair creeping over him, like the time his last tenner went bust on a sure-fire winner at Goodwood and his girlfriend at the time jilted him, all on the same day.

'I think he's overcome, Mumsie. I'll see you later and tell you all about it. Bye.'

Blowing a kiss, Lavinia scooped up her clothes and dived into the bathroom. 'Must dash, darling. Hurry up and get dressed, otherwise Jarvis will be wanting to know what we've been up to.'

Moodily searching for his socks, William wished he knew what they'd been up to, as well.

It was a sadder and wiser William who borrowed his uncle's utility and drove over slowly to the hospital later that morning to break the news. He was so preoccupied with his worries that he drove straight into the concrete sleeper post in the car park. When he got out to inspect the damage, he took in the smashed headlamp and crumpled bumper and knew somehow that this was just a warning signal, a mere passing shot across the bows so to speak, just to let him know there were lots more nasties hanging around over the skyline.

He found his uncle cheerful, despite being bandaged up to the eyebrows and having both a leg and arm in splints.

In answer to William's enquiry about his health, he wheezed, 'Not bad, can't grumble, I suppose, in the circumstances. At least I don't have to sit at home worrying about the bills all the time. What's up with you, my boy. You look as if lady luck's deserted you.'

'You don't know how right you are, Uncle,' brooded William.

'Well, at least we haven't got Lavinia to worry about.' He sighed happily. 'I haven't seen her all morning. Wonder what she's up to.'

His complacent attitude struck William as being grossly unfair. He burst out passionately, 'If you knew what she'd been up to you wouldn't go on like that.'

Lord Beddington opened his eyes in surprise. 'Why what's the matter, what's she done now?'

'What hasn't she done,' said William bitterly, and proceeded to offload all his feelings on the subject, bringing his uncle up to date with the most biting phrases he could muster.

'So,' said Lord Beddington thoughtfully, 'she's got you by the short and curlies, as the saying goes.'

Slightly taken aback by his uncle's graphic way of summing up the situation, William nodded dejectedly. 'You could say that.'

To his annoyance, Lord Beddington covered his mouth to hide a smile, then giving up the pretence he started laughing. 'I'm sorry, my boy. Can't help seeing the funny side of it. Ouch, mustn't do that too much, it hurts.'

'I'm glad someone can see the funny side of it.'

'Look, take my word for it. These things have a habit of sorting themselves out. She's not a bad sort really,' he mused, conveniently forgetting the havoc Lavinia caused in the hospital. 'You'll see, in a few weeks when you've got used to the idea of being engaged you'll look back and have a good laugh about it all.' As William jumped at the word 'engaged' like a startled colt, he patted him reassuringly.

'Come on, you've got to get these things in perspective, my boy. Good Lord, what do you think would happen to our good doctor if he went around worrying about things, like you're doing? Oh, that reminds me, have they sorted out who's going to take over organising the festival, by the way? I suppose it'll be old Doc, seeing that it's a cause so dear to his heart. You might remind him he'd better keep my wife posted on what's going on, otherwise I wouldn't like to answer for the consequences.'

'No, not exactly,' said William, temporising. 'The committee thought it would be a good idea if Dad took over and asked me to contact him.'

'What?' quivered Lord Beddington. 'I hope Doctor Medway put a stop to that.'

'Well no, he supported the idea actually.'

'He what? Why, the weak-kneed, half-witted idiot! I might have known.'

Seeing the look on William's face, he asked urgently. 'You didn't, did you?'

William coughed. 'As a matter of fact, I did. But Dad turned it down flat.'

Lord Beddington let out a great sigh of relief. 'Thank heavens, you had me worried there for a moment. So he's scotched the whole idea? Excellent, excellent.' Then so as not to wound his nephew's feelings, he added hastily. 'Don't get me wrong, my boy. There's nobody I respect more than your father, but I must admit we don't always see eye to eye on how things should be done.' He shuddered at the thought of all those yachts piling up on the mud flats. 'I suppose I'm getting set in my ways. Just put it down to an old man's whim.'

'You don't understand, Uncle,' said William unhappily.

'What else is there, my boy? There's nothing more disastrous than your father taking over. And since there's no danger of that...' He saw William shaking his head and found himself doing the same.

'There isn't, is there?'

'I was just trying to tell you, Uncle,' went on William doggedly. 'After that, Lavinia had a word with him and persuaded him to change his mind.'

'She did what?' shouted Lord Beddington, causing some of the patients along the ward to raise their heads to see what all the fuss was about. 'The little minx, wait till I get hold of her!' His Lordship grasped William with unexpected strength and forced himself to speak in a lower tone of voice. 'What do you mean, *persuaded* him?'

'Let go, Uncle, it wasn't my idea.'

Lord Beddington relaxed his grip slightly and fixed a tortured look on his nephew. 'Go on.'

William pulled his tie straight and tucked his shirt in again. 'She said the Lord Lieutenant told her we were in danger of being taken over by the Reds, and the Council was riddled with them and that Len Bartlett was the worst of the lot.'

'Eh?'

'And that Gerald... the Lord Lieutenant...'

'His name's not Gerald,' interrupted Lord Beddington feebly, beginning to lose the thread of the conversation.

'Look, I'm trying to tell you,' argued William. 'Anyway, she said that when the Lord Lieutenant, whatever his name is, heard that Dad would be able to come and organise the festival he was delighted.'

'He said what? That's plumb crazy. Why, he was the one who booted your father out when he messed up that regatta!'

'I'm only telling you what Lavinia told me. Anyway, he said he would.'

'Who said, who would?' asked his uncle dazedly.

'Dad agreed to come down in two days to take it all over.'

'Oh, my God – what will your aunt say when she hears!' Lord Beddington was appalled.

'With his staff.'

'Where are we going to put them all, and how are they going to be fed... for three whole weeks?' He raised himself with difficulty and caught hold of William's shirt again.

'William, you've got to stop them, you must. You don't understand!'

'Look, Uncle, just calm down. You know what you said about getting things in perspective? In a few weeks you'll look back and have a good laugh about it.'

'Listen, haven't I got through to you yet? I'm stony broke, the whole estate will be finished if you let them in. You've got to help me, my boy. I've tried to tell Edith, but she won't listen.' He ended up shouting, 'If it gets out, I'll be ruined!'

Hearing all the noise, Matron bustled up. 'Mr William, I cannot have his Lordship upset in his present state of health.'

A hysterical peal of laughter erupted from her patient. 'Upset! Listen to the woman! Get these bandages off, I'm getting out of here.'

Matron turned anxiously and caught sight of a row of inquisitive faces peering through the swing doors. 'You see what I mean. He's getting all worked up. It's not good for him or the other patients.' She peered at William as he watched Lord Beddington going puce in face. 'What's the matter?'

'I think Uncle has fainted,' said William simply.

It wasn't until he was driving away that he remembered. He hadn't told his uncle about the broken headlamp and the bent bumper.

5

ONE MESS AFTER ANOTHER

On the morning of the General's arrival the sun shone brightly and even the flowers seemed to be at their best to welcome the idea of visitors. Inside, the news of their arrival went down like a lead balloon. Apart from William, the one who viewed the prospect with most alarm was Jarvis. Even his usual suave composure seemed to desert him. His upper lip positively quivered.

'How many did you say were coming, sir?'

William's reply did nothing to reassure him. 'As well as my father, he's bringing half his staff, as far as I can gather,' he added, kicking at the shingle moodily.

Jarvis swallowed. 'Half his staff?'

'Yes, I've no idea how many. How are we going to cope?'

'I shall do my best. Most disconcerting.' Then his customary sense of service came to his aid. 'Would sir care for a drink while you are waiting?'

'You're darn right sir would. Make it a stiff one, while you're at it.'

'Right away, sir.'

In minutes he reappeared with a folded deckchair and

table. 'If sir would care to take a seat, I will bring the refreshments.'

After a short interval he oozed out again with the necessary items.

William took a quick gulp and sat back relaxing, trying to ignore the other's strange attire, but after a while he felt he had to enquire about the reason behind it.

'I say, er, Jarvis.'

'Yes, sir?'

'Erm, I don't want to be personal and all that, but my father is rather old fashioned and, er, I mean to say, he might find your outfit's not up to your usual, erm high standard...'

'I must apologise for my unseemly attire, sir, but I deemed it best to offer my humble garments to his Lordship in the circumstances and I have not had an opportunity of...'

Whatever the circumstances he was referring to was never enlarged upon, for at that moment the words froze on his lips as an extraordinary cavalcade of vehicles appeared at the end of the drive and made their way towards them.

'Good grief.' William viewed what appeared to be a convoy with mounting astonishment. 'What on earth?'

A despatch rider pulled up in front of them. 'Which way to the car park, sir?'

'Car park?' questioned William feebly. 'What car park?'

The driver waved his hand at the line of vehicles behind him. 'For General Duncan's advance liaison group, consisting of ten vehicles and equipment support unit, sir.'

William turned, bewildered, to Jarvis. 'Do we have somewhere to put this lot?'

'Not as far as I am aware, sir.'

'But this is frightful.'

'Somewhat unfortunate, I would agree, sir.'

Before he could collect his scattered wits, an open tourer pulled up behind with a squeal of brakes and a short stocky figure got out and strode towards them. With a sinking feeling, he recognised the familiar bluff features of his father, followed by his faithful lurcher hound. 'Ah, there you are, my boy. Where's your uncle – has he made the necessary arrangements for our arrival?'

Pulling himself together, William did his best to explain the situation, without much success.

Slapping his leg with his cane, his father grunted. 'Just like him to mess everything up. Well, in that case we'll just have to park in your drive, can't be helped. Better get your man to show us where our quarters are and we'll have a wash and brush up ready for supper, what?'

William coughed. 'How many in your party, Father?'

'Eh, only myself and staff – about a dozen all told, nothing to write home about.'

Sensing a note of anguish by his side, William turned in desperation, seeking support. 'Can we lay on anything in that direction, Jarvis?'

'I fear the problem would be insurmountable, sir.'

'What? You can't do it?' snorted the General in disbelief. 'In a place this size? I don't believe it. Don't bother me with the details. Have a word with my adjutant, he'll be along shortly – he's good at arranging things. Come along, Rufus.' As he turned away, he paused to deliver a parting shot. 'By the way, you do know your fellow's improperly dressed, don't you?'

Taking a fortifying gulp at the drink Jarvis silently offered him after his uncle had departed, William reflected dismally on the situation that was rapidly getting out of hand. As he tried to imagine what on earth his uncle would say at the turn of events he came out in a cold sweat. He was so engrossed in the problem about what he could possibly do next that he failed to take in the presence of a new arrival who pulled up before him on a rusty old bicycle, with a squeal of brakes.

'I say, is this Beddington Hall, what?'

'Eh?' William raised his head with an effort, hoping the apparition would go away and leave him to suffer in silence. 'Yes,' he answered distractedly.

'Oh, good – that's a relief. Sorry I'm late. The old crate packed up on me at the last moment, so I scrounged this old wreck.' Sensing a lack of response, he went on, 'I expect the old man told you I was coming.'

'What... what did you say?' William made an effort.

'Algy Frobisher's the name, Lieutenant Frobisher if you want the full title and all that rot. Most people call me 'Bishy' for short. I'm standing in for Percy, the old adjutant – he's gone sick, poor devil. So you're stuck with me, I'm afraid.'

'I'm sorry,' apologised William, 'we weren't expecting quite so many turning up.'

'That's typical of the old man – always wanting to show off.'

William coughed, slightly embarrassed. 'That's my father you're talking about.'

The other smote his forehead. 'Clang. Sorry, putting my big foot in it as usual. Bang goes my pip.'

'Don't worry,' said William, sunk in gloom. 'He's always like that. It's just that it couldn't happen at a worse time...' Then feeling he ought to explain he added, 'We just don't have the staff to deal with things like this – feeding all you lot, for example...' He trailed off.

'Is that all?' beamed the other. 'If that's all that's worrying you, don't give it another thought – we're loaded with the stuff.'

'What – what was that you said?' A gleam of light flickered at the back of his mind. He looked up hopefully, not daring to believe what he'd heard.

'Absolutely. We've got enough grub to feed an army in the jolly old canteen at the back – we never go anywhere without it, don't you know.'

'Whew! That's a relief – I'd better let my uncle know. He

was getting rather worried about it – especially now he's crocked up in hospital.'

'I say, too bad. Give him my regards and tell him not to worry about a dashed thing. Tell him, the Duncans are coming - that should buck him up.' He cast a glance at the building. 'Lucky devil, owning a pile like this though. I bet it costs a fortune keeping it going these days, what?'

'You can say that again,' emphasised William, nodding at Jarvis behind him. 'Looks as if some of us could do with a decent outfit to go with it.'

'I didn't like to mention it,' observed the Lieutenant with a grin. 'I thought he was going to give us a turn and entertain us. Tell you what,' he exclaimed struck by a sudden thought, 'why don't we get him kitted out from our facilities unit? And while he's there he can rustle up some grub – I expect the old man will be feeling a bit peckish by now.'

'Would you really?' William felt like embracing him. 'I was wondering how we would manage.'

'Think nothing of it. Your man will know where to set it up, won't he?'

'Leave it to Jarvis.' Having settled that point, he put out his hand impulsively. 'By the way, I'm William – but all my friends call me Bill. I say, you're a real brick coming up with all this, like a fairy godmother.'

'Well, I've never been called that before,' guffawed Algy heartily. 'I can see we're going to get on splendidly.' Then recalling his duty. 'I'd better go and let the old man know, otherwise he'll be having my guts for garters, as they say.'

Left to himself, William wasted no more time in letting his uncle hear the good news. But when he got through on the phone, his uncle was only partially mollified and insisted on knowing more. 'How many are there, did you say,' he croaked despairingly, 'and how long are they going to be there?'

William hesitated, 'Can't say – Dad said about a dozen but

don't worry, they've got stacks of food with them, so it doesn't matter how long they're here. You don't have to worry about a thing, honest.'

'But you don't understand.' The voice at the other end quavered. 'The place is not in a fit state – anything might happen. The walls are peeling everywhere. It hasn't been touched for years.'

'Don't worry,' William tried to reassure him again, imagining his uncle struggling to get up at the news and causing mayhem in the hospital, 'I'll look after things. I'll make sure they leave it in a fit state.'

'But they may be there for weeks – you know what soldiers are.'

William did his best to sound practical. 'Now don't get worked up, Uncle – everything's fine. The new man in charge here is a great help. Algy Frobisher is the man. I've quite taken to him. Look, I'll keep you posted, don't worry. I'll ring you every night. Now promise you won't worry.'

'Doesn't look as if I've got any option,' came the weary reply. 'Just make sure they don't pinch all the cutlery... they're heirlooms.'

William sighed exasperatedly. 'Forget it, Uncle. They'll have their own knives and forks.' Catching sight of Algy signalling him in the background, he ended hurriedly, 'Look, I'll speak to you later, right? I have to go now.' Wiping his forehead, William put the phone down and stepped away thankfully, re-joining his new friend.

'You look as if you could do with a snifter,' sympathised Algy. 'Coming up, a touch of what the doctor ordered.'

William took a gulp and began to relax. 'You don't know the half of it. If it's anything like the last time he was here...' he hesitated, but making up his mind after the other's encouraging nods, proceeded to tell about his father's previous visit that resulted in the local regatta fleet piling up on the beach after a disastrous mix-up.

'But in that case, why did your uncle ask him to come back again?'

'He didn't,' groaned William. 'That was because Lavinia persuaded him, blast her.'

'Who's Lavinia?' Algy asked, mystified.

'You may well ask,' replied William bitterly. 'She's the PR woman they got in to publicise this dratted hospital appeal and once she'd spun him a cock and bull story about our Council members being at the back of a red inspired plot, he couldn't wait to take it on.'

'I see,' Algy said thoughtfully, knowing his superior's reputation. 'I suppose it would have seemed like a jolly old red light to a bull.'

'And he's not the only one she's hooked,' blurted out William, without thinking.

'Oh, yes?' His friend cocked an enquiring eyebrow. And then, before William knew it, it all came out with a rush. How he'd got trapped into having supper with her and after forcing a drink on him all he remembered was waking up sharing the same bed, with her practically fixing the date of the wedding.

'Ah, caught by the short and curlies, eh?'

'That's what my uncle said,' remembered William soulfully.

'And he's Lord Beddington? After the title, you think? Got yourself a good lawyer?'

'Maybe.' William could not be consoled. 'And no, I haven't. What am I going to do, 'specially now I've met...'

'Aha – not another fair damsel?'

But William would not be drawn. 'Maybe,' was all he could bring himself to admit.

'Like that, eh? Never fear – Algy is here. Between the two of us, we'll think of something.'

'Wish I had your optimism,' was all he could think of saying.

'Cheer up, I see your excellent fellow is signalling lunch is ready. Shall we join your father?'

'Why not. By the way, look out for the dog, he doesn't mind where he goes.'

'I had noticed, after ruining two pairs of perfectly good shoes.'

As they entered a room that Jarvis had prepared, the General was already voicing his feelings in no uncertain manner about the quality of service.

'Come along, come along,' he greeted them rapping the table. 'Where are you – do I have to wait all night?'

'Sorry, Dad,' apologised William. 'I was ringing Uncle to let him know what was happening and to put his mind at rest.'

'What about my mind, my boy, when I'm waiting to be served? And by the way,' he said tersely as William started apologising again, 'don't address me in those familiar terms in front of the staff, even if I am your dashed father.'

'My fault, sir,' interrupted Algy hastily, doing his best to steer the conversation onto safer grounds. 'I was asking William how he came to get involved in this operation with his uncle – awfully interesting, what? The time simply whizzed by.'

'Never mind about that. What I want to know is how that man managed to let the house get into such a deplorable state. It comes to something when we even have to find his butler, or whatever he calls himself, some decent clothes so's he can go about his duties properly before we can get some food served. That reminds me,' he said breaking off, 'has he fed Rufus yet – where is the hound. Rufus,' he bellowed, 'where the blazes are you?'

At the sound of his voice, the door slammed back and a shape hurtled in, barging into the table and leaping up to lick his master, with unfortunate results. The next moment, the force of his welcome caused the rickety chair the General was sitting on to collapse in a heap, leaving him sprawling amid the wreckage, with the dog enthusiastically licking his face.

'Help me up someone and get that damn dog off me,' he yelled furiously.

As Algy helped him struggle to his feet, trying hard not to laugh at the spectacle, a despatch rider knocked at the door and entered just at that moment to witness the General's discomfort.

'What the devil does the man want, bursting in like this,' he demanded furiously, dabbing at his jacket in a frantic attempt to wipe away the bespattered remains of his meal that clung to him, whilst vainly trying to stop the dog licking it off.

'Sorry to interrupt, sir,' apologised the messenger, pulling the intercom button from his ear. 'Just to report you have a visitor, a Mr Barklett, I think. Says he is from the Council – authority on port, or something.'

'I can't see him now. Get rid of him, Frobisher, I can't see him in this state. Tell him to make an appointment or something. *Do* something, blast it.'

Seeing his friend hesitating, William came to his rescue. 'I really think someone should see him, if it is who I think it is – it may be important. Shall I see what he wants?'

His question remained unanswered. The next minute the despatch rider was thrust aside and Len Bartlett came galloping in, his hand outstretched. 'So you're the new man who's taking over the hospital appeal – just the fella I want to see. I've got just the thing to make it a guaranteed success and get it off the ground right from the start. Now, this marina scheme of mine is a brilliant idea that will not only turn our port into a sure-fire tourist attraction, it will bring new hope to the whole region before you know where you are.'

'Wait a minute.' The General held up to hand to quell the

flow. 'Who the blazes are you, and what d'you mean bursting in like this?'

Not to be put off, the visitor regarded the interruption as a mere trifle to be ignored and went on in full flow. 'It will mean new jobs and bring fresh hope to all those poor devils who've been out of work for months and it will make your name a byword, a name to be proud of by everyone who knows you.'

'I already know who I am,' interrupted the General rudely, 'but who the devil are you, is more to the point?'

Wounded, the other replied somewhat huffily, 'Why, I'm on the Council – everyone knows who I am. Now as I was saying...' He began to wind himself up again, ready for a fresh onslaught.

Unable to get a satisfactory reply, the General turned to the others. 'Who the devil is this fellow – what's his name?'

'Mr Bartlett,' replied William defensively on behalf of Kate's father, hoping to calm things down. 'I think you ought to listen to him. He's very keen on promoting this marina idea of his – it's expected to bring all kinds of benefits to the area.'

'He doesn't sound much of a benefit, as far as I'm concerned,' fumed his father. 'Wait a minute, Bartlett, that name sounds familiar. Where have I heard that name before?' He wheeled around. 'Weren't you in the armed forces at one time, sir?'

'I have that honour,' replied their visitor, taken aback. He added reflectively, 'Though I don't think it was shared by others in the same company I could name...'

'I thought so!' blazed the General. 'Now I know who you are. You're that blasted Len Bartlett who was under my command when I was out in the Middle East. Always stirring up trouble in the ranks, like some blasted barrack room lawyer. Did your best to wriggle out of anything that remotely sounded like doing your duty. Dammit, you're nothing but a Commie. Get out of here and don't come back. Frobisher, see this... man out immediately.'

Afraid his superior's buttons might burst under the strain, Algy took the visitor's arm and politely escorted him out of the room.

'Thank God that bounder's gone.' There was a sudden shout outside and Frobisher re-appeared, trying hard not to grin.

'What was all that about? Now perhaps Jarvis, or whatever your name is, can give me a hand cleaning this mess up.'

'It seems that our visitor trod on another kind of mess where Rufus has been,' offered Algy apologetically.

'Good show – serves the fella right,' beamed the General. 'Well done, Rufus,' he approved, patting the dog's head. 'Just make sure I don't see hare or hound of that menace again.'

6

HER MIND MADE UP

News of the setback weighed heavily on the Bartlett household the next morning.

The sparrows and goldfinches were doing their best to liven things up in the garden, but inside the atmosphere was somewhat different.

Len Bartlett was pushing the odd sausage around on his plate with moody indifference and even the entry of his daughter Kate did nothing to lift his spirits.

'Morning, Dad,' she said lightly, bestowing a peck on his head in passing. 'Where's Mum?' She sniffed. 'And what's that awful smell?'

'She was up ages ago – doing her bit to persuade her W.I cronies to back our marina scheme, fat chance. Oh, and that pong was when I stepped in the blasted General's dog mess yesterday – sorry about that. You've got a job if you want one – my shoes need a bit of a clean-up.'

'Sounds as if it wasn't only the shoes that suffered. You look as if you've had a heavy night of it, out on the tiles.'

'You could say that again,' he agreed, feeling depressed. 'You've heard about that General Duncan character who they've got in to run that hospital appeal with his son, Willie or something?'

'William,' corrected his daughter, her face stiffening up at the mention of the name.

'Well, William then, it doesn't matter,' he said listlessly. 'I called in yesterday hoping to get him to cough up some of the money for our marina scheme and d'you know what – he turned out to be my old C.O when I was in the army.'

'Why that's great,' enthused Kate, 'he'll be able to give you all the backing you want – now you don't have to worry about anything.'

Her father snorted. 'Some hopes. He's the last person I should have asked – we couldn't stand the sight of each other and I don't suppose his boy will feel any different, now he knows.'

'But what did you do to upset him?' she wanted to know.

'Never you mind,' he snapped irritably. 'Down with the masses, that's his sort. You don't understand, love. I've grown up in this neck of the woods and I've seen what suffering causes with men out of work. It's been my one ambition to make this marina idea of mine a success – to bring fresh business and jobs into the area and make the place thrive again.' He paced restlessly up and down. 'We've just got to think of some other way to get some support. There must be something we can do, if I could only think what it could be.'

'As long as you don't ask me to help out. I don't want anything to do with him,' she said shortly.

Len Bartlett's head jerked up, light dawning. 'That's it – why didn't I think of that before? You're just the one I can rely on to pull it off for your old dad.' At her lack of response, he persevered. 'Why, I seem to remember, you two youngsters got on like a house on fire after you met him, didn't you?'

'That was before I heard those rumours that he's been

playing around with that Lavinia woman,' she retorted. 'Why should he be interested?'

Her father laughed it off. 'Why, that's just a boy and girl affair – he'll grow out of it. They all do, believe me.'

'And according to her mother, they're getting married. She's after his title, Dad, everyone knows about it.'

Len puffed his cheeks out and tried again, hopefully. 'It won't last darling, believe me.'

'And they've been sleeping together. It's no good, Dad – I can't do it. Don't ask me.'

'I didn't know you cared.' He stopped short, taken aback at her attitude.

She stamped her foot and declared angrily, 'I couldn't care less.' She turned her head away and fought to hide her feelings.

'Hey, what's the matter, love?' He got up to console her and she bowed her head, brushing away her tears.

'I hardly know him,' she managed with an effort, 'and yet he seemed so different when I met him, not like anyone else I've ever known.'

'I'm sorry, I shouldn't have asked you, but...' He hesitated.

'But – what, Dad?' she questioned, concerned at his attitude.

'If you must know,' he admitted heavily, 'and it'll all come out sooner or later. The fact is... I've put all my money into getting this marina business off the ground, and if it doesn't come off I stand to be ruined.'

'Dad – why didn't you say? If only I'd known.'

'I didn't want to worry you, love.' He patted her head.

She shook her head impatiently. 'Forget what I said, Dad. What can we do about it?'

He held her close and looked over her head sombrely. 'I wish I knew. If there was something about that old port of ours that could save us...'

'Of course, there's only that old legend about buried

treasure on some Spanish galleon they used to talk about,' she recalled doubtfully. 'But everyone knows about that – it's just an old wives' tale.'

'Wait a minute,' he exclaimed, suddenly revived. '*They* don't know about that – they've only just got here. It might be worth a try and I know just the man to lead the hunt – someone I met down at the docks the other day, Captain Borshak. He tells me he's done all this type of work before. Why don't we go for it – that man Duncan was always dead keen on money, I seem to remember.'

'If you think it's worth it, Dad.' Kate straightened up determinedly and pushed a curl back into place, her mind made up. 'I'll see what I can do.'

'That's my girl.' He ruffled her hair gratefully. 'Now we're getting somewhere.'

Meanwhile, despairing about his ability to deal with the situation at first hand while he was stuck in hospital, Lord Beddington was doing his best to lever his heavily bandaged leg out of bed, whilst trying to persuade Matron that he was fit enough to leave.

But he met his match with that determined lady. Nobody had dared to question her authority in St. Mary's before and she didn't intend any patient to start flouting her decisions now, despite his exalted rank. As quick as a flash, she was at his bedside and thrust a thermometer in his mouth to quieten him down, whilst calling on the assistance of a bevy of nurses behind her to put him back where she considered he belonged.

'Now, my Lord, you know all this excitement is not good for you. You'll have all the other patients upset – what would Lady Edith have to say if she knew?'

'Gugg—ggg- phlew,' he gasped, expelling the offending article out of his mouth at last with such force that it hit Matron in the eye. 'That's better, take that thing away – there's nothing wrong with me. I must get back. You don't realise what they may be getting up to while I'm away. The place is falling to pieces; it's in a terrible state.'

'So will you be if you don't behave yourself, my Lord,' she admonished severely, wiping her face disdainfully and handing the remains to the nearest nurse for disposal. 'D'you wish me to tell her Ladyship all about it?'

'No, no... by no means,' he added hastily. 'All I want to know is how long do you propose to keep me here, that's all I want to know.'

'Weeks and weeks,' came the smug reply, aware of the added prestige her two patients were providing. The very thought of it gave her an inward glow of satisfaction.

Lord Beddington groaned. 'You don't know what you are saying. What am I going to do while I'm stuck here?'

'Why don't you make yourself comfortable and I'll get the nurse to bring you a nice cup of tea... with your favourite chocolate biscuits,' she added persuasively.

Satisfied she had won her argument for the time being, she nodded at the nearest nurse before making for the rest room to repair any damage to her face that might require attention, a priority everyone knows is so essential to restore one's authority.

Accepting the situation with resignation, Lord Beddington lay back wearily and pondered over the bleak prospects staring him in the face. As he closed his eyes to shut out the unending problems that were queuing up waiting to be heard, he asked himself feverishly what fresh disasters could possibly happen. *All I need now is for that blasted Cuddles woman and Lavinia to get in on the act,* he thought despondently. *The next thing we know, they'll be taking over the hospital appeal and if they make a success of it, with that wretched Lavinia behind it, she'll be after Edith's job on the Council as well and I'll never hear the last of it... and I won't be there to stop them either.* He brooded on the nightmare it conjured up if Edith came to hear about it. He shuddered at what it might lead to.

That's not all, he groaned to himself. *Once she's made it and she's crowned Chairman, she'll be there for keeps... and if Lavinia lands William as well, I'll be expected to conjure up a wedding present... and the next thing we know, she'll want to spend her honeymoon at the Hall... and I'll be expected to do it up, after all his men have finished pulling it apart...* The hideous possibilities were endless. Jerking upright at the frightful vision it presented, he came to an instant decision. *There's only one thing for it. I must get William on the phone right away and tell him I want to see him urgently – before it's too late.*

Elsewhere, Lavinia was not one to leave the grass to grow under her feet. She believed in following things up in true PR fashion. As soon as she heard about the General's arrival, she was on the phone to her mother gleefully.

'Mumsie, now's our chance to get in on the act, and do old Len Bartlett out of a job,' she added, knowing her mother's ambitions in that direction.

'Why, what's up, darling?' Her was mother was on the alert. 'What's the latest?'

'Get this.' Her voice oozed suppressed excitement. 'I've just heard through the grapevine that your old enemy Len has been given the boot after trying to wheedle some loolah out of the General for that crummy old marina scheme of his.'

'No, what happened?'

'It turns out that our friend was a pain in the neck while he was serving under the General when they were out in the Middle East together in the last dust up... they were at loggerheads all the time and couldn't stand the sight of each other apparently.'

'Excellent,' purred her mother. 'So how does that help us?'

'Don't you see? With old Bedders and his wife out of the way in hospital, now's the chance to get well in with the General and fix up my wedding settlement from him, nudge, nudge... and get you lined up as the next Chairman of the Council.'

'How soon can we see him?' was the instant response.

'What's wrong with this afternoon, Mumsie. How are you fixed?'

'Give me a chance to put my make-up on, darling, and I'll be right with you.'

Sparing no expense, Lavinia hired a car and chauffeur and in less than half an hour they were being escorted to the front door in style.

Peering out of an upstairs window where he was sprucing himself up after getting over his recent unfortunate accident, the General hastily put on a coat, making sure the stains were removed, and rang the bell for Jarvis. 'Who are those people outside?' he enquired testily. 'Anyone would think it's a royal visit.'

'A Mrs Muriel Fox Cuddles and her daughter Lavinia, sir.'

'Lavinia, that rings a bell – where have I heard that name before?'

'I understand the young lady in question has been in touch with you on the telephone recently, on behalf of Master William, to enlist your support in aid of the Hospital Appeal, sir.'

'Ah yes, I knew I'd heard it somewhere before. Well, you better show them in.'

'I've taken the liberty of escorting them to the reception room, sir.'

'Right – oh, and Jarvis...'

'Sir?'

'You'd better rustle up some tea and things.'

'I have already spoken to the Catering Sergeant, sir.'

'Good. Then tell them I'll be down shortly.'

'Very good, sir.'

After straightening his tie and taking a last look in the mirror, General Duncan made his way downstairs to be greeted by his beaming visitors.

'General Duncan, what an honour to meet you,' she simpered. 'Everyone is talking about you, as I'm sure you must be aware. Allow me to introduce myself. I am Mrs Muriel Fox Cuddles and this is my daughter, Lavinia, who I understand has already been in touch with you.'

'Pleased to meet you, Madame,' he replied politely, beginning to thaw at the compliments being bestowed. 'How can I help you?'

'It's not a question of how you can help me, oh no, perish the thought. We are here to offer you our united support in combatting the dreadful influence that certain members of our Council are doing their best to bring about to undermine our society.'

'And who might that be?' he asked hopefully, almost anticipating the answer.

'Why, I thought everyone knew that – it's that awful man, Len Bartlett, who else?' Before he could add his own pungent views on the subject, she went on breathlessly, 'In my own small way, I have been leading a fight to overcome this dreadful influence – if I might say in due modesty – as a not unknown personality in our little community. I come from a fighting stock that stands up for our rights and human dignity, don't you agree. You may have heard of the Fox Cuddles of the Norfolk branch, going back to the Norman times? But of course, we make no claim for personal fame, our duty comes first, as you might expect.' Before he could get a word in, she rushed on, 'And you must have heard about the success of my daughter, Lavinia here, who is now a leading public relations consultant,' and she added coyly, 'and who has recently been delighted to accept a proposal of marriage from your splendid son, William?'

Waking up after being almost overcome by the non-stop flow, the General found himself offering his congratulations in a bemused kind of way. Already the atmosphere was becoming more cordial, minute by minute, and by the time Jarvis appeared with the life-saving refreshments relations were reaching an all-time high as the General found himself listening to the identical views he had already expressed at length. In short, it was soon becoming a virtual love-feast.

Unaware his friend's fate was about to be sealed, Algy was bending his mind to thinking up ways of helping William out of the unholy mess he was in, but as each possible plan came up for consideration he was forced to dismiss it out of hand as being unrealistic. In short, he was beginning to admit to himself that William was in the soup, up to his neck.

He was about to give up and instead seek out William and try to console him when a soft voice broke into his consciousness.

'Excuse me, can you tell me where I can find Lieutenant Frobisher?'

He looked up and blinked. In front of him stood a young girl who seemed to have just stepped off a heavenly cloud to bring instant sunshine into his life – in short, a real corker.

'Er... yes, that's me. How can I help you?'

Looking suitably demure after specially dressing for the occasion, Kate traced out a pattern in the dust with her daintily shaped shoe.

'I'm so glad. I hope I haven't disturbed you in your duties.'

'No, no,' he stuttered, 'I'm completely free – how can I help?'

'I'm told that you know General Duncan awfully well and

that he relies on you for all kinds of useful advice, and I was wondering...'

'I dare say he sometimes listens to what I have to say,' he replied modestly.

'That's not what I heard.' She smiled appealingly. 'You see, it's like this...' As she unburdened herself, he listened with increasing foreboding about the reason for her mission. Touched by her anxiety about her father, he wondered as her tale unfolded if her suggestion about the possibility of a treasure trove might possibly influence the General, knowing his keen interest in acquiring the latter in any shape or form, following his well-known gambling habits in the officers' mess. While he turned the matter over in his mind, his lack of immediate response was misinterpreted by Kate who added impulsively, 'I'm sorry to come to you like this, but I've got nobody else I can turn to – it's not as if I can ask William.'

'Ah,' he exclaimed enlightened, 'you don't happen to be the young lady he was telling me about? I hope you don't mind me mentioning it but I understand that he's awfully fond of you.'

'That's not what I've heard,' she interrupted coldly. 'His affections are fully engaged elsewhere, I understand.'

'Wait, I can assure you that's not true,' Algy insisted. 'He's explained all about that little... erm,' he coughed, 'accident.'

'Is that what you call it?' cried Kate heatedly, forgetting herself for a moment, 'I don't believe it.'

'It's true, every word of it – that Lavinia, it was all her doing,' came a despairing voice behind them and turning she came face to face with the last person she expected to see.

'You!' was all Kate could utter and turned away blindly, anxious to leave.

William stood in her way, summoning up his courage, determined to have his say. 'I swear to you on the bible,' he declared passionately, 'since I met you, nothing else matters. I've got to say it – I love you, Kate. You mean everything to me.

Don't believe all those stories you've heard – they're not true. It's all a pack of lies. Don't turn me down – I can't go on without you.'

'I say, I think this is where I should leave you,' interposed Algy hastily. 'Young blood and all that.' But the others were so wrapped up in their declarations it was doubtful if either of them heard.

Overwhelmed by his entreaties, Kate wavered. 'How can I believe you when I'm told you... slept with her.'

'I tell you, I only had that supper with her out of politeness when she was persuading Dad to help with the hospital appeal. I didn't know she was going to slip a Micky Finn in my drink. The next thing I woke up and found we were in the same bed together. It was a put-up job – her and her mother between them. I wouldn't marry her if she was the last woman on earth. Ask anyone.'

Algy coughed discreetly. 'Here's your chance to find out, old lad. Your father's just seeing them off the premises.'

William turned sharply in bewilderment and Kate gasped. In the distance, General Duncan was saying farewell in a genial manner to Lavinia and her mother as they left, waving goodbye and blowing kisses.

Catching sight of them, the General made his way briskly in their direction. 'Ah, there you are. You've just missed meeting a charming couple, my boy. Oh, of course, you know the young lady, I keep forgetting. I tell you, you seemed to have found just the right one this time at last. Lavinia Fox Cuddles – what a gorgeous popsy and according to her mother, related to half the leading aristocracy in the country. You certainly know how to pick them. I was happy to assure her I was willing to stump up, despite the current shortage of cash. I didn't realise how expensive getting married is these days. Never mind, I expect we can chivy something out of the hospital appeal fund, if it takes off.'

Taking her in for the first time, he turned hospitably to Kate. 'I'm sorry, I didn't notice you had a guest – where're your manners, my boy.'

Recovering with an effort, William swallowed and made a hasty introduction. 'Sorry, this is Kate... er... Bartlett, an old friend.'

'Bartlett? No relation to that pesky Len Bartlett, by any chance?'

Kate took over, smiling coldly. 'I'm his daughter – how do you do.'

The General carried on unabashed. 'I suppose you can't help it, young lady.' Struck by a sudden thought, he unbent a trifle. 'Tell you what, you'd make quite a decent bridesmaid, how about it?' Adding confidentially to William as an aside. 'Not a bad idea that – all helps to keep the costs down. You'll know all about that when you get to my age, my boy.'

It was the last straw. Kate drew herself up and decided she'd had enough. Tossing her head, she turned on her heel and strode off. William rushed after her, appealing to her in vain.

'Did I say something?' General Duncan turned to Algy, mystified. 'What was all that about - there's no satisfying some people.'

7

BURIED TREASURE

Turning William's problem over in his mind the next morning, Algy was distracted by a whispered aside as he left the breakfast table.

'Excuse me, sir. Can I have a word?' It was the Catering Sergeant, looking slightly embarrassed.

'I'm sorry, have I forgotten to settle up?'

The man shuffled his feet nervously. 'No worries on that score, sir. Your slate's clean – always is.'

'Then what's the problem – are we running out of supplies or something?'

The Sergeant twisted his apron and swallowed. 'No, nothing like that...'

'Come on, Ted, you can tell me – what's up?'

'Well sir, it's not my place to mention... I wondered if you might have a word on my behalf.'

'Cough it up – I'll do what I can, you can trust me, after all the time we've served together.'

There was a sigh and the words came out with a rush. 'It's the General, sir. His mess bills are sort of... overdue, like.' He leaned forward and whispered in Algy's ear.

'Good heavens, as much as that?'

'Yes, sir, and that's only last month.'

Algy heaved a sigh. 'Let me have them and I'll see if I can have a quiet word about it.'

A look of relief spread across the other's face and he mopped his brow.

'You're a real gent, sir. Don't know how to thank you – here they are.' He pulled a roll of bills from a pocket in his apron and handed them over. 'Wait a minute.' He checked his other pocket and found another crumpled roll. 'I think that's the lot.'

'I should bally well hope so,' commented Algy, eyeing them without enthusiasm. 'I'll see if I can catch him after the morning briefing. He's going to love this lot.'

'Better you than me, sir,' said the Sergeant thankfully. 'I'll stand you a round next you're passing, if you feel up to it.'

'I might well need it, Ted.'

'Thanks a million.'

His fears were well justified. To say that the General was not amused was missing the mark by a couple of continents. When it came down to it, Algy would have willingly undertaken a ten mile route march with full army pack to avoid such an encounter.

'This is outrageous!' spluttered the General when he got his voice back, his eyes popping out of his head at the sight of the total. 'I can't have spent that much – it looks like the National Debt. I'll have the Mess Sergeant on a charge for this... it's preposterous... they must be forgeries.'

'They do seem to have a signature, sir.' ventured Algy.

'Hrm, so they do,' the General acknowledged reluctantly, as the steam stopped coming out of his ears. 'What the devil am I to do?'

'You could pay it back in instalments, sir, say over a few months.'

'On my pay? More like a couple of years. I'd need a gold mine to pay for this lot.'

Fragments of an earlier conversation he had with Kate struck a chord with Algy. 'It's funny you should say that, sir, but...' he hesitated.

'But what, man? Out with it,' demanded the General, clutching at straws.

'There is that story of young Kate's she came out with yesterday. It sounds fantastic, of course...'

'What story? Don't keep it to yourself, man. Spell it out.'

'It's funny you should mention about goldmines, sir. Apparently, there's a story running around about an old Spanish galleon waiting to be discovered by some lucky merchant along the coast somewhere near here. Just an old wives' tale, I expect.'

'Oh? Why should that young lady be interested, I wonder,' pondered the General, stroking his jaw pensively. 'Might be worth following up to see if there's any truth in it.'

'Someone already has,' volunteered Algy. 'The spies tell me that our old friend Len Bartlett is convinced it's in the local bay. He's trying to raise funds for that marine project of his in the hope he'll earn himself a fortune finding the wreck. Said to be full of pirate treasure, I gather,' he added casually.

The General's eyes gleamed. 'Why didn't I hear about it?'

'We've only just arrived, sir,' Algy pointed out reasonably. 'Do you want me to find out whether there's anything in it?'

'Yes, of course... No, wait, we don't it to sound too official, otherwise I'll have that confounded man on my back again. Have a quiet word with William.'

'Of course, sir. I'll see what I can do.'

The General took another look at the pile of debts. 'And don't take all day about it – make it top priority.'

Algy smiled contentedly to himself. 'Understood, sir. I'll get onto it right away.'

. . .

Musing to himself, he made his way to the butler's pantry where he sought out Jarvis for first-hand information. 'Ah, Jarvis, just the man,' he called out cheerfully, 'Any idea where I might find William?'

His enquiry, however, evoked a sombre response.

'I could not say exactly, sir. It is hardly my duty...' then he unbent at the sympathetic approach. 'All I can say is that I am profoundly disturbed at his present state of mind.'

'What's up, Jarvis? Has he got a touch of the blues?'

'I am not entirely cognisant of the phrase you used, sir. But if I understand your meaning correctly, he did strike me to be somewhat despondent. I might even say extremely despondent – quite unlike his usual cheerful manner, I might say.'

'Well, tell me where I can get hold of him, old chap, and I'll see if I can cheer him up. Where's he got to and all that rot.'

'I could not say precisely, sir, but the last time saw him he told me he was going for a walk.'

'Did he say when he would be back?'

Jarvis shook his head doubtfully. 'I fear not, sir.'

'Where was he heading?' Algy prodded him gently.

'He said he was going to the headland overlooking the bay.'

'Right-ho, I'll see if I can catch him.' He turned to go. 'If I get lost, what's the name of the spot?'

Jarvis moistened his lips. 'They do say it's called "lover's leap", sir.'

As the news penetrated, Algy gulped and hurried off. Hailing a despatch rider outside, he jumped in the passenger seat. 'Make it snappy, Harry, this is an emergency. I need to get to the headland overlooking the bay – d'you know the area?'

His driver pulled out a map. 'Where do you want to go, sir – has it got a name?'

Algy adjusted his goggles grimly. 'Lover's leap.'

Revving up, his driver put the map away. 'It's a bit steep just there – I'll do what I can.'

True to his word, he deposited Algy at the foot of some steps leading up to the summit.

'Good man.' Heaving himself up, Algy clambered up the hill where he stumbled across William sitting slumped near the edge. Trying to sound casual, he greeted his friend heartily. 'Ah, that's where you've been hiding. I wondered where you'd got to. What's up, old fellow?'

Looking up dully, William heaved a weary sigh. 'Was that you making that confounded noise on a motor bike? I thought I had the place to myself.'

Relieved that he'd got his attention, Algy sat down beside him. 'What a splendid view from up here, what? I say, steady on,' he grabbed hold of William's arm to stop him looking down at the dizzying drop below, 'you nearly went over the side there, old chap."

'Well, why not,' said William gloomily. 'There's not much point in going on now.'

'What's up – girl trouble?'

William gave a hollow laugh. 'What other kind is there? That blasted Lavinia's got her mother to put a notice about our so-called engagement in all the paper and Kate won't even speak to me.'

'Here, calm down, Bill... you don't mind me calling you Bill?'

William brushed aside the question gloomily. 'Call me what you like, Algy, it's not going to make any difference – I'm for it.'

'Never say that.' Algy tried to lighten the mood. 'All is not lost, you've got me to help you.'

'Oh yes?' A note of bitterness crept into his voice. 'How can anyone help me now?'

'Let's be practical. Just think, why is Lavinia so keen to tie the knot?'

He tried to put it tactfully. 'Have you got any expectations, as they say?'

'Only blasted wedding bells.'

'No, what I mean, old chap, is... your dad, is he rolling in the stuff or have you got any aged relatives in the offing?'

'I see what you mean. Dad's only got his army pay and he can't wait until Aunt Emma pops her clogs.' He gestured, waving his hand. 'She lives in the family shack, a mouldy old castle up in Scotland somewhere.'

'And this Aunt Emma – is she good for a few beans?'

'Oh, she's well off, all right. But she's mad as a hatter. Never know what's she's going to do next. Wouldn't be surprised if she left it all to a dog's home.'

Algy let out a gratified sigh. 'Why, there's your answer. You can bet your bottom dollar that this Lavinia of yours is thinking ahead and has you down as her meal ticket for the big life. All you have to do now is to prove her wrong.'

'And how do I do that? She and her dratted mother are all set to announce our wedding plans and Dad's all for it. He thinks her family's connected with half the landed gentry in the country and must be loaded. Besides,' he added, without much hope, 'even if I got out of that, there's not a hope that Kate will come round. She won't even speak to me.'

'Ah, well I think I may have something up my sleeve that will help to correct that point of view,' said Algy, helping him to his feet. 'Cheer up. Just leave it to your Uncle Algy.'

Before they parted back at the house, Algy got out his notepad. 'That reminds me, where do I find this Kate of yours? Have you got her number written down somewhere?'

But William didn't need to look anything up. He rattled off the number as if it was engraved on his memory.

Patting him on the back after he had stowed the information away, Algy encouraged him. 'Be of good cheer, old lad, I'm on your side. You never know what we can do now I'm on your case. Have no fear, the news I have to impart to that young lady will no doubt be guaranteed to bring a smile to her rosy face and a sparkle to her eyes.'

Leaving his friend with a doubtful expression, Algy repaired to the nearest phone and settled back in his seat, mentally crossing his fingers.

'Am I speaking to Miss Kate? Good. This is Lieutenant Frobisher. Yes, we met the other day. I wonder if I might trespass on your good will and have a quiet word with you? I think you will find it worthwhile. What's it about? It's about that little matter we were talking about recently... hello? Are you still there... yes, your father's fascinating plans for that marina project. Where? Shall we say at the Horse and Groom in half an hour. In the private bar? No, just the two of us. Excellent. Good-bye.'

'...so you see, young lady, anxious as I am to help you, it must be understood that this is all entirely unofficial. My master, the General, cannot be seen to express an interest in the venture, however attractive it might seem. If you could give me something to go on to back up your father's claim,' he looked around cautiously, 'that there is evidence of treasure to be found, it would make a fantastic difference. You do see that?'

'Of course.' Kate traced a pattern on the table with her glass. 'I know there's some talk of a map.'

'Yes?' encouraged Algy, his interest quickened. 'Could you get hold of it or let me have some details – anything like that would help.'

Kate put her glass down and looked at him squarely in the eye. 'I might, but tell me honestly, why are you getting involved in all this? Is it anything to do with... William?'

Algy accepted the implied rebuke sheepishly. 'Not directly. I am, as you were, acting on orders on this occasion. But anything I can do to bring you two young people together, I would do most willingly. Now that I have come to know William, or Bill as he lets me call him, I feel almost like an elder brother to him, don't you know.'

'Then perhaps you can explain your 'brother's' recent extraordinary behaviour,' she remarked coldly.

Algy reflected. 'I know it may sound damning if you accept all the rumours going around, but after Bill explained it to me I believe every word of it.'

'You men,' she said scornfully, 'you're all the same – you all stick together.'

'If you had seen him when I came across him this morning about to throw himself off the cliff edge, you wouldn't say that, young lady,' he replied severely. "Lover's Leap", they call it.'

She caught her breath. 'You don't mean that – you're only saying it.'

'If Jarvis hadn't told me where he was going, in time," Algy admitted soberly, 'I might have had a different story to tell you.'

Kate sprang to her feet, hand to mouth. 'Oh Bill, where is he – is he hurt?'

'No, only looking pretty foul. Hemmed in on all sides, you might say.' He looked at her hopefully. 'He might feel better if you went and told him how you feel.'

'I can't bear it – where is he?'

When they got there, Algy couldn't resist listening to the ecstatic greeting and the first 'You poor darling,' before closing the door gently on the two love birds. Suffice it to say that he was extremely gratified at the resulting reunion. Giving them time to make their feelings abundantly clear to each other, he checked his watch after ten minutes and tapped on the door before entering. The sight of Kate nestling in Bill's arms was the answer he was hoping for and brought a beaming smile to his face.

'Oh, Bill, can you ever forgive me? I should have trusted you.'

'You were quite right, my darling,' argued Bill stoutly. 'I should never have let that Lavinia anywhere near me in the first place.'

'No, you shouldn't have, precious, you weren't to know.'

'If I'd have known what she was like, I would have run a hundred miles to get away from her. I'm a first-rate idiot.'

'No, you're not. You're my own sweetheart baa-lamb.'

'Now that we've established it was nobody's fault,' interrupted Algy tactfully, 'aren't you forgetting something? I hesitate to remind you, but Bill's engagement to the lady in question has already been announced in all the leading papers and both Bill's father and Lavinia's mother seem intent on the event going ahead.'

Bill and Kate looked at each other and spoke simultaneously. 'Never!'

Speaking for both of them, Bill said defiantly, 'We'll run away together and get married – they can't stop us. That's what we'll do – eh, darling?'

'Quite right, precious,' then hesitating slightly, she added firmly, 'they can't stop us.'

'And if I might be so bold as to ask, what do you propose to live on?' enquired Algy delicately.

"Why, Dad will rally round once he knows how things stand,' asserted Bill defiantly, 'and so will Kate's', he added fondly. "Won't he, darling.'

Clutching his hand for support, Kate admitted reluctantly, 'I'm sure he would... if he was able to.' Then she broke down. 'I should have told you, dearest, he's put so much of his own money in this marina scheme of his that it's left him without a bean.'

'Oh, well,' said Bill, taken aback, 'I'm sure Dad will come up with something.'

'I hate to disabuse you, old lad,' interrupted Algy sadly, 'but your dad is in rather a similar position.'

'Eh? What d'you mean.' Bill couldn't believe his ears. 'Dad must have salted away a packet over the years from his pay – you're talking nonsense.'

Algy sighed as he revealed the painful truth. 'You wouldn't say that if you'd seen the size of his Mess bills.'

'But he couldn't have owed that much.' His young friend was not convinced.

'I'm afraid it's true – I've seen the size of his debts. The Mess Sergeant showed me them this morning.'

'But-but.' Bill floundered. 'What about Aunt Emma – can't she help him out? She must be loaded.'

'I may be wrong, but from what your father was saying I gather she has rather decided views on the dangers of alcohol to which he seems addicted.'

'By George, I believe I did hear something of the sort.' He looked around desperately. 'What the hell are we going to do?'

'There is possibly only one solution I can think of that might appeal in this situation,' said Algy thoughtfully.

"What's that?' His audience both pounced on his words hopefully.

Algy turned to Kate courteously. 'I gather Bill's father was showing an interest in the possibility of investing in this exploration project of your father's, Kate. Purely as a commercial venture and entirely unofficial, you understand. I gather his pollical views are diametrically opposed to those of your father.'

'Yes,' agreed Kate, bewildered. 'But if he's broke, where is he planning to raise the money?'

'Yes,' put in Bill. 'He hasn't got a hope, from the sound of it.'

'I understand it would be more in the nature of a last fling of the dice,' agreed Algy. 'That is why he is anxious to have some sort of guarantee about the chances of success.'

'I know he's potty about it.' Kate chewed her lips doubtfully. 'I'd do anything to help him, of course – the silly darling only told me about the fix he's in the other day.'

'I believe you were talking about the existence of a map,' reminded Algy persuasively. 'That might make all the difference.'

'I'm sure we could come to some sort of an arrangement about getting his backing, darling.' Bill gave her arm a squeeze.

Making her mind up, Kate let go of Bill reluctantly and stood. 'I'd better see if I can get hold of that map then.'

After she left, the mood lifted for a moment as they discussed the situation.

'Bless her, I knew she'd come up trumps,' Bill said devotedly.

'I don't wish to dampen your chances, but haven't you forgotten something?'

Bill glanced up with dawning apprehension. 'Of course, Lavinia.'

'Yes, it wouldn't surprise me if she isn't in touch with your father right now to fix up the date of your nuptials and all that rot. You see if I'm right.'

8

GETTING THE SHOW ON THE ROAD

But William didn't need to check up – Lavinia was already on the phone. Not one to miss a trick, she was soon purring down the phone to her nearest and dearest.

'Mumsie, don't you think it's time you gave the signal to get the show on the road?'

'Patience, my darling,' cautioned her mother. 'There are one or two things I need to get fixed up first.'

'But Mumsie, I thought we had it all cut and dried – what's the hold-up? I need the go ahead so I can organise the bridesmaid and my special outfit for the occasion – you know the one. I can't wait to see the dress designs.'

'You don't realise, pet. This is just the chance I've been waiting for. At last I shall be able to get that old stuffed shirt of a general to let me handle the Hospital Appeal and what is more important – get him to nominate me for Leader of the Council, before Lady Edith gets out of the hospital, confound the wretched woman. I hope she doesn't get the chance. I've got Matron on my side, thank goodness – the publicity is just what she's been dreaming about. Don't go and spoil it all for me at this stage, I implore you.'

'I get it, Mumsie, but don't leave it much longer in case William finds some excuse to wriggle out of things. He's beginning to get that hunted look I was telling you about. I've got a nasty hunch he's still hankering after that Kate Bartlett creature. I don't want to give him a chance – I wouldn't mind betting he'll look for any excuse at this stage.'

'Don't be ridiculous, my love. You know very well he hasn't got a hope in that direction – Roderick can't stand the sight of that left wing father of hers. He'd rather die. I know his sort – he thinks there's a Commie hiding around every corner, waiting to take over.'

'Well, put a shift on, Mumsie. Strike while the iron's hot is my motto.'

'Leave it to me, we've got a Council meeting tonight. That might be just the opportunity I've been waiting for. Wish me luck.'

'Oh I do, Mumsie.' She had a sudden thought. 'It might be an idea to offer to pay for the reception – I always find something like that can help to sway the deal.'

'Thank you, darling, I'll bear that in mind. Now I must get on, otherwise I might miss that all important Council meeting and I've never missed one yet. I'll ring you later, when I hope to have some news.' Satisfied that she got all her priorities sorted out, she rang off.

Directly the meeting was over she bore down on the General with gay determination before he could find an excuse to escape.

'Oh, there you are – just the man I want to see,' she cooed. 'Why don't we have a nice cup of tea and a little chat, just the two of us. I've got so much to tell you. Don't tell me – you can't wait to get away from our little Council meeting. I know how it is.' She laughed roguishly, waving a finger at him. 'These things must be a terrible bore for you.'

'No, no, not at all,' he lied feebly, longing for a pint of

refreshing beer in the safety of the Officers Mess, where he could begin to relax and try to think up ways of paying off his massive debts. 'How can I help you?'

As he said it, he realised he had made his first fatal blunder. If he had any sense at all, he should have made for the hills as soon as he saw her approach with that purposeful expression. He knew where he stood where men were concerned. If any of his own lot had something to complain about it had to be in writing, and then the man would be wheeled in, standing to attention, with a guard on either side. Permission to speak, sir. That was the right and only way to go about it. It was what he'd come to accept and he knew how to deal with it.

However, with the fair sex, it was a different matter. He would quite happily exchange banter with the best of them at the odd cocktail party or two. But whenever he was asked to do something, like the Vicar's wife calling for a donation as had sometimes happened in recent years, he knew he could always rely on his late wife, Letty, to give him the support he needed. 'Be firm, Roderick' she would always insist and he invariably followed her command faithfully and it never failed.

But with Muriel Fox Cuddles, he realised directly he clapped eyes on her that he was facing a more formidable adversary, who would be happy to break all the conventional rules of etiquette to get what she wanted. And he could see by the determined look on her face that she couldn't wait to get started.

'It's not what you can do for me, dear man,' she boomed majestically, 'quite the reverse, in fact. Now, here's a cosy spot, why don't we park ourselves down. Just right.' She steered him into an alcove and signalled the waitress. 'Tea and a few of your delicious little iced cakes, Margaret. Now then,' having got that sorted she put on her charm offensive, 'dear man, I expect you're wondering what on earth this is all about. I couldn't help thinking when you were sitting there looking so noble and self-sacrificing and willing to put up with all our petty little affairs, how you managed to get mixed up in all this boring business in the first place. No,' she patted his hand reassuringly, 'you don't have to pretend with me. You don't mind if I call you Roderick, do you? General Duncan sounds so terribly formal and stuffy. Good, you can call me, Muriel.'

She patted his hand again, taking his assent for granted. 'Now, I'm sure you have so many other more important things to worry about, so I'm proposing to take some of those boring old duties off your hands, so you don't have to worry about them any longer.' Imagining they were coming up to the first fence in the Grand National, she gave his hand an extra squeeze of assurance before squaring up for the jump off.

'You can't begin to imagine how utterly tedious and time consuming some of these local affairs of ours can be. Take that silly old Hospital Appeal, for instance. Spending your valuable time trudging around forever and a day, trying to whip up support for yet another worthy cause, I ask you, when there are masses of volunteers around who are simply aching for the opportunity to take it off your shoulders. Honestly, wouldn't you rush at the chance to hand it over?'

'Well, naturally, when I think of all the other duties that I'm blessed with...' he began tentatively. Her triumphant cry that greeted his acceptance swept over him like the familiar tidal wave that he remembered vividly from their last visit, leaving him feeling dizzy and overcome, unable to contribute anything more to the subject under discussion, let alone make a decisive comment, even if he tried.

By the time she had finished and was beaming at him as if bestowing a coveted benediction, he gathered that he had been released from the admitted time consuming job of gathering support for the Hospital Appeal – a task he was more than willing to hand over. But at the end of their one-sided conversation, he found to his bewilderment that he had also relinquished his temporary role as Leader of the Council.

Before he could muster up enough strength to protest or even comment in any shape or form on the turn of events, she was already dismissing the matter as of little importance and proceeded to get down to the main subject on the agenda. Grabbing hold of him as he attempted to make an excuse to leave, she proceeded to concentrate her attention on the all important issue in hand, determined to thrash it out despite any possible opposition, as if she was astride the winner in the last race of the day, and was expecting to get to the finishing point before anyone else and receive the coveted prize. 'What I really wanted to talk to you about is this matter of Lavinia's engagement. I haven't heard anything more about it from either of them, the naughty children,' she began, crossing her fingers. 'Not to put too fine a point on it, he hasn't got cold feet, has he?' She gave a little tinkling laugh as if the very idea was too absurd for words.

'Of course not,' denied Roderick hastily, to avoid another avalanche of mind numbing speculation and possible incrimination. 'He... can't wait for the day, I am sure.'

'I know,' she exclaimed as if the thought suddenly occurred to her, 'in that case, why don't we celebrate the occasion? What fun. Why don't we do just that? We could get all our friends to come along and help us fix a date. It's no use leaving it to the children – they have no idea. Let me see, we could make it a special event – a Springtime Ball, now how's that? Everyone could dress up for the occasion and I know just the place – The Regency Palace, just off Knightsbridge.'

'Um, I know it's a special occasion, but wouldn't that be rather expensive,' he hedged, 'perhaps the local hotel would be more appropriate?'

'Oh, don't be such a killjoy, you naughty man. It's not every day your only son gets married, is it?'

'No, of course.' He hesitated, thinking of his massive Mess bills and how she expected him to pay for it.

'You don't have to worry about the cost,' she reassured him, seeing the expression of mounting panic on his face. 'I'll look after all that side of it – consider it my treat.'

He licked his lips and made a weak attempt as if to try and persuade her but she waved aside his protests, pressing his arm fondly. 'After all, now I know we're such good friends, it's the least I can do.'

Before he could steer the subject onto safer grounds, she dabbed an eye delicately with a wisp of handkerchief and sighed artistically. 'It's such a comfort to know I have a good friend at last to turn to since my Herbert was taken from me.'

'You mean, he was kidnapped?' The General's mind grappled with all the possibilities.

'No, you id...,' she nearly forgot herself and stopped herself just in time, 'dear man', she substituted. Taking a deep breath, she added with a convincing sigh. 'No, the good Lord said his time was up and he had to leave me all on my own to face the world, whatever the cost,' omitting to mention that her late husband had picked a moment when her back was turned to run off with the babysitter at the first opportunity. She shook off the unpleasant memory, as if swatting a troublesome fly, and laid a possessive hand on his arm. 'Now I have my reward,' she smiled archly, 'a new and dear friend to advise and comfort me.'

As the significance of her remarks began to sink in, the General hurriedly consulted his watch and scrambled to his feet. 'A thousand apologies, dear lady. I've just remembered. I have a most important engagement I had almost forgotten. I'll leave all the details in your good hands to arrange. Let me know what you decide.' Wiping his forehead in relief, he called out 'Taxi!' before he had even reached the exit.

· · ·

As soon as he got back to his quarters the General helped himself to a large whisky, drank it down in one gulp and hastily poured another. He sat there blinking with a slightly bemused expression and after he had got his breath back reached out a shaking hand to ring for his adjutant.

'So you see the ghastly situation I've got myself into, what am I going to do?' he appealed desperately. 'The thought of having that woman as my son's future mother-in-law is appalling. Come on, Frobisher, think of something.'

'Right-ho, sir.' Turning the problem over in his mind and debating how he could turn the unexpected news to the best advantage for his friend William, Algy meditated for a moment on the possible alternatives, an action that only served to irritate the General still further.

'Well, don't just stand there, think of something.'

Algy coughed diplomatically. 'Sorry, sir, I was just reminding myself of several other factors that we should take into consideration.'

'What other factors, dammit. What could be worse than things as they stand?'

'I was just getting my thoughts in some sort of order, sir.'

'Well don't keep them to yourself – spit them out.'

'Perhaps sir is not aware that the situation has changed somewhat since last we spoke?'

The General clutched his hair. 'Don't say that there could be anything worse – what factors are you drivelling about?'

Abandoning his coughing routine that seemed to infuriate his superior, Algy felt his way delicately. 'I feel I ought to tell you, sir, that your son, William, has confided to me that his affections have become engaged elsewhere.'

The General grunted dismissively. 'Silly young fool. Not another of his romantic flings – I don't believe it. He'll have to change his tune now where Lavinia is concerned. She won't let him go in a hurry if I know anything and nor will her mother if she gets to hear about it.' He shuddered at the thought.

'I fear it's not just another of those flings, as you so admirably put it, sir. If I might bring you up to date on the current situation. The lady in question is young Kate, Len Bartlett's daughter.'

'What, you're not serious? How the hell did that happen? I thought I made it understood that any contact we made with that family was to be purely financial and on a confidential basis? Surely I made myself abundantly clear on that point.'

Algy was about to agree that William was in full agreement with the idea but realised his flippancy would not be well received, so he changed his approach.

'I don't think young William saw it that way exactly. It all happened so quickly.' He went on to explain his friend's dilemma. 'It was not through any fault of William's,' he began cautiously, gaining confidence as he eyed his superior. 'When Miss Bartlett saw how welcome Lavinia and her mother were received by your good self she kind of blew her top, as the expression is, and refused to have any more to do with him. But William became so overwrought at the idea of losing her he was almost driven to distraction and threatened to end it all by jumping off the cliff.'

He waited for a note of understanding, but getting a blank stare he carried on gamely. 'Luckily, Kate got to hear about it,' at this point his voice gathered strength as he began to lay it on thick, 'and rushed to saved him in the nick of time and after an emotional and frank discussion, they fell into each other's arms and decided there and then...' He stole a glance to his superior, anxious to see how his story had been received so far.

'How the devil do you expect me to know what they decided. What happened next?'

'Seeing his efforts were wasted, Algy put on a satisfied air of benediction.

'They decided then and there that whatever the future held in store they were determined to get married as soon as possible.'

'I dare say,' commented his father, unmoved by the rhetoric, 'but where does that leave me?' he asked plaintively. 'I've just left Lavinia's blasted mother to make all the arrangements for announcing the wedding date.'

Battling on, Algy switched topics in a hurry. 'The other... er... factor that needs to be considered, of course, is your own... um... financial situation, sir.'

'That's no problem,' interrupted the General. 'Lavinia's mother has agreed to pay for the do, thank God.'

'I fear we're talking at cross purposes, sir,' reminded Algy gently. 'That's only the start of it. I believe you were also anxious the last time we spoke of searching for some way of supporting Mr Bartlett's marina project, should it prove a viable proposition, as a way of adjusting your recent, ahem, financial aspects to a more favourable position.'

'Oh, good Lord, I'd forgotten.' He tried to brazen it out. 'I thought I told you to find out about that?'

'I did, sir,' Algy assured him. 'It appears that there exists a map that will hopefully help us to locate the position of the sunken vessel in question.'

'I know, you told me. Did you manage to get hold of it?'

'I am happy to report that Miss Kate is willing to procure a copy for us to examine, sir.'

'Well what the devil are we worrying about. That's excellent news, Frobisher. Well done.'

'Ahem, I should add that her co-operation is contingent on one condition.'

There was a pregnant pause as the General examined the matter briefly.

'What's that – I expect they'll want a damn great commission for the privilege?'

'I expect that would be a matter of negotiation, sir. If I may explain.'

'Well go on, blast you.'

'I understand that the young lady is perfectly willing to do so... on the understanding that you give her father full support to his marina project.'

'But I can't do that officially when I don't know whether it's worth it,' cried the General, appalled. 'What would that Fox Cuddles woman have to say if she hears about it – she hates the sight of him.'

'In such a situation, I would imagine that she would have to get used to the prospect, sir, however dire, in her estimation.' Algy allowed himself a faint twitch of the lips, adopting Jarvis's more restrained response. 'More to the point, I'm afraid there is one final stipulation.'

'Don't say there is more?'

Giving his superior a look of sympathy mixed with compassion, Alfie dealt the final blow. 'On this last point,' he said anxious to get it over, 'she insists that you give them your full consent to their marriage, sir... and William fully supported her on this issue.'

9

THE NIGHT OF THE BALL

'He did what? The young idiot!'

'Naturally, he was anxious not to jeopardise your financial prospects if the marina project proved satisfactory, sir,' Algy reminded him consolingly.

'Oh, I suppose not. But where does that leave me – still under an obligation to that blasted Fox Cuddles woman. I can't satisfy both of them at the same time. The whole thing's intolerable. Don't just stand there – think of something.'

'If you would leave me to handle the negotiations, sir, I think I might be able to find a way out of the dilemma,' offered Algy hopefully, doing his best to strike a note of cautious optimism.

'I damn well hope so. Carry on, Frobisher, and don't spend too much time over it. Any moment now that blasted woman will ring me up to fix a date, knowing her. She's not one to let the grass grow under her feet.'

On cue, the phone began to ring and the General jumped like a cat on a hot tile roof. 'Answer the thing,' he ordered peevishly. 'Tell them I'm out.'

'Hello? General Duncan's residence? Good morning,

madame. No, I'm afraid the General is not available just at the moment. He's in a meeting. Yes, I will, certainly, madame. I'll see that he gets that message. Thank you for letting him know. I'm sure he will be highly gratified.'

'Well?' demanded the General. He mouthed the word fearfully, expecting the worst.

Algy nodded in silent confirmation. Clearing his throat, he repeated the message like someone announcing the departure of a dear friend. 'That was Mrs Muriel Fox Cuddles, sir. She thought you might be pleased to know that she has booked the event in question for Saturday evening at 6 o'clock in the Green Suite at the Regency Palace.'

'Saturday evening? Why dammit, that's tomorrow,' he groaned and looked around wildly. 'What have I done to deserve this? This needs thinking about – give me a drink.'

'Your usual coming up, sir,' replied Algy obediently. Thinking about the problems lying ahead, he reached out for another glass thoughtfully. 'I think I'll join you, if I may.'

Fulfilling her promise to let her daughter know what had been decided, Mrs Fox Cuddles couldn't wait to break the news.

'Why, Mumsie, that's great,' she whooped gleefully. 'I'll wow them all with my midnight blue number – you remember the one. That'll teach him.'

'Don't overdo it, darling,' her mother cautioned. 'It's not a coming out event like that last one when I had to cover you up with my dressing gown. I think that pink velvet would be more suitable. You don't want to upset the guests.'

'If you say so, Mumsie.' Lavinia sounded disappointed for a moment. 'Anyway, it's one in the eye for that Kate Bartlett – we'll be able to really splash out and make it something they'll all remember.'

'Don't forget I'm paying for it,' reminded her mother, coming over faint at the thought.

'Never mind, Mumsie, now you're in charge at the Council you can claim it all back on expenses.'

'So I can.' Her mother brightened up. 'I never thought. That would give that stuffy old Roderick something to think about, if he only knew.'

But General Duncan had other, more pressing problems to think about. Item one, how to persuade William to fall in with his wishes and accept the unpalatable news.

'But Dad, you can't ask me to go through with it – you know I love Kate and nobody else – certainly not Lavinia.' He shuddered. 'Anyone but her.'

'Look here, my boy. I've never asked you to do anything for me before, but this is really important, otherwise I'll never get that Fox Cuddles woman off my neck. It's just this one night,' he pleaded. 'Just think of it as only a social occasion, then when it's over you can forget all about it.'

William looked incredulous. 'Only a social occasion? How can I forget about it, when they're going to use it to announce the date of my marriage – to Lavinia? Talk sense, Dad. What d'you think Kate will have to say about it? She'll hit the roof – and I don't blame her.'

'Do it for my sake, just this once, that's all I ask you.'

'Not even once and that's definite, Dad. I'm sorry, but you're asking the impossible.'

'Oh, I give up. Have a word with Frobisher – see if he can knock some sense into your head.' He turned and strode out wrathfully, calling out for his adjutant as he went.

A few minutes later there was a discreet tap on the door and Algy poked his head in. 'The old man asked me to have a few words.' He cocked his head enquiringly. 'Okay to intrude?'

'Willian turned wearily. 'Oh, it's you, Algy. Things are in a hell of a mess, I expect you've heard. He wants me to go to this gala night in London so they can announce the date of my wedding to that wretched Lavinia woman.'

'Tough luck.' Algy looked sympathetic. 'That's just like the old man, taking the easy way out. Mind you,' he said thoughtfully, 'when you come to think about it, it may be a blessing in disguise, if you look at it another way.'

'Oh, come on,' said William sarcastically, 'you're beginning to sound just like the old man. Why should I do it for his sake – it's my life and Kate's that's more important at the moment, not a question of his pride, for heaven's sake.'

'Look, I'm on your side, Bill – remember? Just listen for a moment.'

'Okay – but you'd better make it good.'

'Well then.' He marshalled his facts. 'We're all agreed that you and Kate should get married – that's our number one priority, right?'

'That's what I kept telling him, but he wasn't interested.'

'Right, we've got that established. Now fact two, your dad badly needs some help to pay off his Mess bills and the only way he sees a chance of solving that problem at the moment is to back this Marina scheme of Bartlett's in the hope of discovering some treasure.'

'It sounds half-baked to me, but I suppose there's a faint chance of that happening,' conceded William reluctantly.

'It's a ten to one certainty that once he gets involved in that, word will get back to Lavinia's mother and the whole idea will be squashed – she'll see to that, knowing how much they love each other. Right?'

William nodded resignedly.

'And why are they so confident? Because they think your dad will be next in line for a fortune when your Aunt Emma goes, of course. That leaves your dad between the devil and the deep blue sea. Whatever he decides, it's bound to be wrong.'

"So what am I supposed to do about it,' cried William in frustration.

'It's up to us to see. If we can manage to persuade them that he won't get a sniff of that legacy, he'll get Lavinia off his neck before he knows where he is and he'll be free to concentrate on that treasure.'

'And just how do we do that?' demanded his friend, bewildered.

Algy winked encouragingly. 'Leave it to me – if I can't solve that simple little task before the end of Saturday night, I'll turn in my pips, you'll see. Now if you believe me, go and tell your dad and put him out of his misery.'

It was a smart but strangely muted trio who boarded the train to London the next evening, half afraid of what they might expect – William looking anxiously at Algy for support, followed by his father, General Duncan, intensely relieved that the event was actually taking place. By the time they reached the ornate and imposing entrance of the Regency Palace, the General had perked up considerably, fortified by the thought that whatever happened before the evening was over he would not be expected to foot the bill.

When their presence was announced they were informed that their host, Mrs Muriel Fox Cuddles, had not yet arrived. As soon as they had been seated in the entrance lounge, General Duncan took the opportunity of ordering a large Scotch to give him strength to face the ordeal ahead, while Algy accepted a cocktail and William settled for a cider under the watchful eye of his father.

Just as they were beginning to relax, their peace was

shattered by a fanfare of trumpets issuing from the entrance hall.

The General was so startled by the noise he nearly choked on his whisky. 'What the devil?'

There was a flurry of activity and in swept their hostess. 'My dears, I hope I haven't kept you waiting? Are they looking after you?'

'Splendidly, my dear,' assured the General, getting to his feet with difficulty and bowing gallantly. 'Delighted to see you again. You know my son, William, of course,' and he nodded at Algy as an afterthought, 'and my, ahem, adjutant, Lt. Frobisher.' He looked around nervously. 'And your daughter, is she with you?'

'Yes, of course,' trilled their hostess, displaying an expensive looking fur coat before handing it to a waiter. 'She is just powdering her nose. Ah, here she is.'

Timing her entrance, Lavinia swept in and completed a pirouette to show off her latest exotic creation. 'There now,' beamed her mother proudly, 'doesn't she look enchanting, eh William?'

'Er, yes, of course,' said William politely.

'Now,' suggested Muriel Fox Cuddles meaningly, 'why don't you two go and enjoy yourselves on the dance floor while we oldies settle down and watch the fun, eh, Roderick? And perhaps your man would like to see to the drinks?'

Algy rose at the hint. 'I do have a call to make as it happens – if you'll excuse me, sir?'

The General nodded reluctantly, afraid of being left defenceless and at her mercy. 'Don't be too long, Frobisher,' he begged in an aside. 'Remember, we have that little matter to go into.' He raised his voice. 'There's always something to attend to, my dear,' he apologised to his hostess. 'These despatches follow me around everywhere, I'm afraid.'

'You don't have to apologise, dear man. What you need,' she

said nestling down comfortably in the chair beside him, 'is someone to take all those cares off your shoulders.'

Acting promptly at the warning signs, the General felt for his mobile feverishly. 'Heavens, is that HQ again? They never let you alone – excuse me, my dear.' He hoisted himself up to answer it and caught sight of Algy bearing down with the drinks. 'Ah, there you are, Frobisher. Look after Mrs Muriel Fox Cuddles will you, while I attend to this enquiry. Sounds rather important, I'm afraid.'

General Duncan was just congratulating himself at getting away so promptly when he ran smack into a solid looking uniformed officer emerging from the lift, who gave a whoop of surprise at the sight of him.

'Why, durn it, I don't believe my eyes – it can't be. My old friend, Rodders.'

Blinking, the General clutched at his old wartime friend. 'Damn, it's Bugsby. If you only knew how glad I am to meet you again, after all these years. Let me buy you a drink.'

The other reluctantly pulled himself away. 'Gee, I'd love to, Rodders, but I'm already late for an appointment, gosh darn it. Say, are you around the next couple of days? Why don't we make a date – must be over ten years or more.'

'Sounds great to me – where are you staying, Bugsby? How can I get in touch with you?'

'Why I'm staying right here, my old friend. Give me a rain check but make it soon – I've got so much to tell you. Gee, it's just like the good old days. Shoot, is that the time? I must dash. Here, grab my number.'

Scribbling a note on his cuff, Duncan scratched his chin, wishing he could have prolonged the chance encounter, and looking round furtively dived into the Gents, hoping his absence would not be noted.

· · ·

Meanwhile, thinking up something to say to cover the loss of her prey, Muriel Fox Cuddles turned towards Algy, hoping to find out some new and interesting facts about the General that she might store away and use to her advantage on some future occasion. 'Do tell me,' she gushed. 'I expect you're awfully thrilled to be working for someone like Roderick... I mean, General Duncan. I get so used to calling him that – we're such good friends, you know.'

'So I understand, Madame.'

'I am sure you must be full of lovely tales of his generosity and unfailing kindness to his men that you're dying to tell me about,' she encouraged.

Remembering his superior's frequent outbursts on parade in the past, Algy smiled inwardly at the unlikely vision and allowed himself to unbend a trifle. 'Yes, the chaps never stop talking about it. Of course, it's only natural, seeing what kind of man he is... even when he is facing times of tragic adversity.'

'Do go on,' she prompted eagerly.

'Oh, I not sure it's my place to say.' He hesitated fractionally on purpose.

'Poor man, you can trust me – it won't go any further, I promise. Do tell.'

'Well, as long as you treat it confidentially.' He bowed his head solemnly. 'Of course, he's never been the same since his wife passed away, but what hit him most was the breakdown of his Aunt Emma. She was the apple of his eye, you know. It wasn't because she was so well off, financially speaking, of course.'

'Of course,' agreed the other, getting excited. 'Is that the one who lives in that Castle with oodles of mon... I mean servants to look after her?' she added hastily.

'Yes, when she's allowed out,' he started saying, then clapped a hand over his mouth, as if realising his gaffe. 'Oops, I mean, when she feels better.'

'There's nothing wrong with the poor lady, is there?' she asked anxiously.

'No, she's perfectly fit and all that – in her good periods.'

'What about... when she's not so good?'

Algy sighed. 'Well the doctor's very hopeful... she might last for years... we all hope so.'

'Is she well provided for... I mean, does Roderick have to look after that side of things?'

Here, Algy found he had to be truthful even though his imagination was running riot. 'No, she is certainly well endowed.'

He heard her expel a sigh of pent up relief. 'Oh, I'm so glad – for her, of course.'

'Mind you, I understand she is a trifle eccentric.'

'In what way?'

'She has this mad passion for animals. Really weird, if you know what I mean. Keeps on threatening to change her will, so I'm told. Sorry, are you all right? You look a little pale.'

'No, no, it's getting a little warm in here.' She swallowed, fanning her face with an effort. 'I've just remembered I meant to have a quick word with Lavinia – she gets in an awful state in the heat. If you'll excuse me, Lt...'

'Frobisher,' he finished for her. 'I quite understand. Would you like me to find her for you?'

'No, don't bother, I will go – it's no trouble. The walk will do me good. I need some fresh air, it's so close in here.'

After she'd gone, Algy sat there, feeling well satisfied at the way things had gone and happy to think he had done his bit in rescuing William at the eleventh hour.

The next moment, his mood of contentment was shattered at the entrance of an elderly lady demanding attention. Simultaneously, Lavinia re-appeared looking agitated in the arms of her mother, followed by a mystified William and lastly by General Duncan himself.

At the sight of the newcomer, he looked astounded. 'Why, Aunt Emma, what are you doing here?'

Catching sight of him she bridled. 'And why shouldn't I be here when my only nephew is thinking of getting married?'

'Why, Aunty, how are you,' asked William awkwardly. 'How nice to see you. We didn't expect you to travel all this way just for a private party, did we, Dad?' he appealed, confusing everyone by looking at Algy pointedly for an answer.

'What do you mean, William – this is not just any old party,' protested Lavinia, anxious to put the record straight. 'This is to announce our wedding, silly.'

'A sort of family get together, don't you know,' attempted Algy trying to lighten the atmosphere. 'Isn't that so, sir?' He turned to the General for support.

Avoiding the pitfall, the other stammered. 'Did you come down here all by yourself, Aunty? Isn't there someone to look after you?' *At your age was that wise,* was the unspoken thought he had in mind.

'Stuff and nonsense,' she retorted. 'There's nothing wrong with me – I'm as fit as a fiddle. I came down on the overnight sleeper and some idiot of a taxi driver took me to the wrong hotel. Said he thought I was a Lady Worthington, I ask you – not that I wouldn't like to be one, of course. But it's a bit late now at my age.'

'Oh, but I'm sure anyone would take you for one,' gushed Muriel Fox Cuddles, seizing the opportunity and rushing forward to welcome her. 'I don't think we've been introduced. The General is a dear friend of mine,' she explained. 'Come into the lounge and let's get to know one another properly. Let me see, you probably haven't come across our family being so far away up in Scotland. We belong to the Northumberland branch of the Fox Cuddles line... no doubt you've heard of us. Oh yes, we can trace our line back to the Middle ages, or even further I expect. After you, my dear, no, perhaps you'd better let me help you. Where are you, Lavinia dear, take the other arm, that's right.'

'That's torn it. What do we do now?' William said wretchedly.

'This is a turn up for the books,' agreed the General heavily. 'Any ideas, Frobisher? You promised us you could sort it out.'

'I must say I hadn't anticipated this setback,' admitted Algy thoughtfully. 'Wait a minute, something she said just now has given me an idea. Can you prise that Aunt Emma of yours away so I can have a quiet word with her?'

The General and William looked at each other questioningly. 'Go on, William, go and persuade your Lavinia to have another dance and I'll see what I can do with her mother.'

'She's not my Lavinia,'' William started to protest but at a look from his father got up moodily. 'All right, I suppose I must, but don't take all night.'

Eventually, Aunt Emma appeared, looking ruffled. 'What's this all about. Just as I was getting to find out what that nice lady was saying about her ancestors. I found it so interesting. Now what did you want to see me about that's so urgent?'

'I thought as you were getting on so well with Mrs Fox Cuddles and her daughter just now that you might like to know about one of their family's closely guarded secrets that very few people know about, but don't hesitate to stop me if I'm presuming in any way,' hesitated Algy disarmingly.

Intrigued, Aunt Emma sat up alertly. 'Not at all – I am extremely interested. But how do you come into it, young man?'

'As General Duncan's adjutant I get to hear all kinds of secrets in the family – all of it very confidential, you understand.'

'What kind of secrets do you mean?'

'Ah, I can see that I can trust you with a sort of sacred trust that's been handed down from one generation to another?'

'You mean, just like Mrs Fox Cuddles' ancestors?'

'Exactly that.'

'Good, I can't wait for you to start.'

'I don't suppose you've ever heard that there is a special club in the family, a kind of exclusive inner circle with extra privileges of a social nature that most people would give their right arm to join, if they had the chance.'

'Really, how unusual. What do you have to do to become a member?'

'I have been sworn to secrecy, but seeing you're already a member of the family, so to speak.'

'How exciting. You can trust me. I promise not to breathe a word to anyone.'

'Right, well this is the procedure,' explained Algy, trying to keep a straight face. 'This might sound silly, but everyone has to follow it without question. Are you ready?'

'Yes, I'm ready.' Anxiously, 'It won't hurt me or anything like that, will it?'

'No, I promise you. All you have to do is to walk up to Mrs Fox Cuddles and say, without moving a muscle, 'I'm leaving all my money to animal welfare.'

'Is that it?' Doubtfully, 'How strange.'

'That's what everyone says,' assured Algy. 'But the great thing is to look deadly serious as if your life depended on it, otherwise it's no good.'

'How odd,' mused Aunt Emma. 'When's the best time to do it then?'

Algy looked at his watch. 'The sooner the better, before they think of leaving.'

'You will be there to say, if I get it wrong?'

'Of course – I'll be with you all the way.'

Five minutes later, Aunt Emma announced to her stunned audience the sworn password.

Muriel Fox Cuddles stood like a frozen figure, for once unable to respond. After the remark sank in, she quavered, 'Is that so, how interesting!' then promptly fainted and had to be helped away by Lavinia, looking stricken.

Some time later, after Aunt Emma had been escorted back to her hotel to collect her belongings before allowing herself to be persuaded to stay with the General, William managed to corner Algy and asked him furtively, 'What on earth did Aunt Emma say to you afterwards that left you looking so goofy?'

Algy answered simply. 'She said, "How did you know?"'

10

TRUST ME

'You mean,' gasped William at the news, 'you didn't just get her to say it, she really means it – Dad doesn't get a bean?'

'It rather looks that way,' admitted Algy thoughtfully. 'My gambit turned out to be just a lucky guess, by the sound of it. Unless she makes a habit of changing her will, although she didn't strike me as the sort who would. It rather puts the damper on things for your father, I imagine. This calls for another bout of thinking.'

'You can say that again,' said William, utterly dispirited. 'It puts the kibosh on everything. Bang goes any chance I had of getting married to Kate with Dad's help. Where's he going to get his money from now?' A sudden thought occurred to him. 'At least it kills off any hopes that Lavinia had – I wonder what she'll have to say to that?'

Lavinia, it turned out, had rather a lot to say in the circumstances, but it wasn't suitable for publication. After she had run out of steam and her mother managed to get a word in edgeways, she was almost speechless.

'I thought you said she was loaded? After all my efforts...'

'Now don't get excited, darling, how was I to know?' Her mother reflected, 'Perhaps it would have been better if you'd have got that manservant of theirs to bring you a cup of tea that morning – then we would have had a witness.'

'Well I didn't,' snapped her daughter peevishly. 'I'll remember to pack a camera next time.'

'Now, it's no good flying off the handle, darling. Don't give up too soon. Why don't you leave it with me to see what I can do. I'm sure there must be some way around it. That Aunt Emma might be in the habit of changing her will quite often, if the truth was known, according to what that young adjutant was telling me.'

'That's not much help to me, is it?' came the plaintive wail down the line. In that case, she might leave it all to that blasted lurcher hound of his next week. If something doesn't turn up soon,' she decided recklessly, 'I think I might even get in touch with Chuck again, I hear he's just been posted over here.'

'Now, don't let's be too hasty,' her mother cautioned, 'he's only an airman. Where did you say he came from, Arizona or somewhere in the back woods? That's not really one of the top money centres, is it? Cows and things.'

'No but his pa owns an oil well, so he tells me.'

'I've heard about those sort of stories before, darling. Don't let's be too hasty. Now you just sit tight till I find out a bit more, promise?'

'Oh, all right, Mumsie – but don't take too long, otherwise I'll have to start sending all those lovely wedding presents back.'

'Never do that, whatever you do,' her mother implored earnestly, speaking from experience. 'Believe me, I've been there, I know about these things. Trust me.'

On an optimistic note, she reminded herself, 'I've still got Roderick on my side, after I took all those tiresome jobs off him. Now's it's payback time and it's about time he realised it.'

. . .

Back in his study, as he reached out blindly for another lifesaving snort to revive him, the General was still reeling from the ghastly situation he found himself in. As he wrestled with the problem, a well remembered phrase his old English teacher was always fond of quoting came back to haunt him. What was it about... oh yes, "The slings and arrows of outrageous fortune." Well, they certainly seemed to be pointing in his direction. After hearing that death sentence passed by his Aunt Emma last night at the party, he saw no way out from the desperate straits he now found himself in. His only hope now was to call for his faithful adjutant and see if he could come up with any last minute bright ideas.

Before he could press the bell to summon him he heard a tap at the window, followed by a frantic hand waving and a beaming face peering in, telling him in no uncertain terms that his fate was already about to be sealed.

'Hello, dear man. I just happened to be passing and I thought I'd look in and see how you were.'

The shock of seeing her so soon again left him feeling quite weak. 'Mrs Fox Cuddles, how... um... nice,' he managed feebly.

'Yes, I knew you'd be pleased to see me. No, don't get up,' as he levered himself up gamely, trying to get away from her overpowering wave of scent. 'I'll come and sit by you, nice and friendly, like the last time. I thought it was the best way to tackle it, as we've always got on so well together. Now, it's about that silly mix-up over your dear boy William and my Lavinia, and that upset over their marriage plans.'

Outside, Aunt Emma was about to knock on the door to see if he wanted a cup of tea when she heard the tail end of the conversation and intrigued, paused to listen unashamedly.

'I thought if we talked the whole matter over we'd be sure to find a simple solution. You're such a sensible man.'

Help, he prayed to himself. *Where are you, Frobisher, just when I want you.*

'You see, dear Lavinia is such an impulsive child. Instead of talking the matter over calmly, the silly girl is threatening all sorts of idiotic things like...'

The General clutched his head. 'Like what?' he asked, feeling trapped.

'...like bringing a case against dear William for breach of promise... I know,' pressing his arm understandingly, 'these children get such silly ideas in their heads, there's no stopping them, I ask you.'

'But – but, can't you persuade her?' he gulped, aghast at the news.

Mrs Fox Cuddles gave a helpless laugh. 'As if I didn't try... but she takes after her dear father, so unpredictable. I ask you – what am I going to do with her?' she said, shooting a quick glance to see how he was taking it. Satisfied, she decided to apply the knock-out blow. 'And of course, being such an expert on press relations she'll no doubt be anxious to tell her side of the story, as soon as she gets the chance. I do hope you'll come up with something I can say to stop her, dear Rodders.' She started fanning herself. 'I feel so weak and helpless about it all, being such a silly old woman.' She leant forward and touched his hand possessively. 'Of course, if I had a big strong man like you to look after me like my late husband – always there when I needed him – it would make all the difference. Oh dear,' she said, peering down as the General slid off his chair. 'I do believe he's fainted.'

At her words the door burst open and Aunt Emma rushed in to rescue him, ready to defend him in his hour of need. She gazed down at him anxiously. 'What have you done to the poor boy?'

Brisling at the implied criticism, Mrs Fox Cuddles drew herself up haughtily. 'I beg your pardon. I was just having a cosy chat with my old friend – I don't know what came over him, I'm sure.'

'So it seems,' Aunt Emma remarked coldly. After absorbing the veiled threats she'd just overheard, she no longer regarded their visitor as a heaven sent opportunity to gain access to her previous devoutly wished goal of a higher social status. In short, she no longer wanted to have anything more to do with her.

Hearing her robust defence, the General cautiously opened one eye, feeling relief wash over him at the timely intervention, then prudently closed it again.

'I'm sure I don't know what you mean,' her visitor replied frostily. 'I was merely passing on a message from my daughter, Lavinia. I knew it would interest him – I know he holds her interests close to his heart, dear man.'

'So it would seem,' repeated Aunt Emma, making shooing motions towards the door. 'Thank you for your concern. I think you may safely leave his welfare in our hands, Mrs Fox Cuddles – now that I'm here to look after him.' She sniffed suspiciously. 'There's a terrible smell of alcohol around here – I trust you haven't been encouraging the poor man. No wonder he's feeling under the weather. I can't abide the filthy stuff.'

'No indeed,' agreed Mrs Fox Cuddles, lying virtuously. 'I only take it for medicinal purposes myself.'

His aunt's words came as a death knell to the General, who was already dying for a quick snifter to get over his frightful visit, wishing he'd hidden his treasured hoard away out of sight beforehand.

Unfortunately, his resolution came too late. As soon as his aunt had escorted their visitor to the door she returned to lock the front of the drinks cabinet rather pointedly and pocketed the key with grim satisfaction. 'Now, a nice cup of tea is what you want, Roderick, dear – not one of those nasty drinks, urgh. I expect that Mrs Fox Cuddles put you up to it, her and that

Lavinia of hers. I should steer clear of that lady if I were you, threatening William with breach of promise indeed – I've never heard of such a thing. He's well rid of her in my opinion. I'll go and put the kettle on while I think of it.'

'Um, while you're at it, Aunt, perhaps you could leave me that key. I've just remembered something I meant to get out – my diary,' he added hastily, on the spur of a moment.

She wagged her finger at him. 'I know all about you and your excuses, Roderick dear. You don't have to tell me any more of your taradidles. The moment my back's turned you'll be helping yourself to another of those sinful drinks. You were just the same when you were a toddler – always thinking up some excuse or other before getting up to mischief. You'll be far better off doing without it, take my word for it. I'm going to put you on a strict diet from now on, while I'm here. It'll make a new man of you, you see if I'm right.' With that, she stalked out of the door, leaving him drumming his fingers on the desk in sheer desperation, gasping for a quick one to get over the shock.

So that's the situation, Frobisher,' he explained with a haggard face when he finally got hold of his adjutant. 'What the devil am I to do? I'm gasping for a drink,' he added piteously.

Silently, Frobisher offered him a hip flask and waited until the life saving properties started to get to work.

Wiping his mouth at last with a deep felt sigh of relief, the General came to a decision. 'That's better – you'd better get in a ready supply of these while we've got the chance.' He passed a hand over his face wearily. 'But you've heard what she said. How am I going to last out without my rations? She might be here for weeks. She'll be watching me all the time, day and night. You don't know her like I do.'

'If I may remind you, sir, there are one or two other, more pressing problems to consider.'

'I know, you don't have to tell me – how are going to deal with Lavinia, to start with.'

Algy coughed. 'Well, no doubt that young lady is under the misapprehension that you will be able to personally meet the cost of any action she may wish to bring to salve her pride, not appreciating your current liquidity problems.'

'You don't have to spell it out, blast it.'

'It all comes down to whether you feel justified in backing this exploration scheme that,' he tactfully left out reference to Len Bartlett and substituted, 'that young Kate is proposing, which if successful would solve all your problems.'

'How can I do that when I've only got her word that it exists?'

'If it's any help, sir, Kate has managed to get hold of this old map that apparently shows approximately where the Spanish vessel went down.'

'Let's see.' His superior examined it carefully. 'Um, not very precise, is it.'

Algy hid a grin. 'I don't suppose the ship's captain had much time to work it all out. I gather he was caught in the middle of a storm when it happened.'

'Hm, you say her father is convinced about its authenticity?'

'He's sunk all his money into it, she tells me. It's left him without a sausage.'

The General's eyes took on a crafty expression. 'In that case he'd accept any offer we might come up with.'

'Do you wish me to take the matter any further, sir? I gather William and Kate's future is also rather dependant on the outcome.'

'No, we'll wait a bit, it won't do any harm to let that man sweat a bit after all the trouble he's caused me in the past. Now fill that flask of yours up – I'll probably need a dozen or so before I've finished.'

But as the days wore on it wasn't Len who sweated. After strenuous effort to discover where Aunt Emma had hidden the key without success, the General's health began to suffer as he pined for his usual evening tot of whisky. Then on top of it all Algy had an unexpected accident, falling off his bicycle, and was confined in hospital with a fractured leg.

Robbed of his ready supply of sustaining nourishment, the General grew more and more morose and irritable and snapped at everyone who crossed his path. As soon as he managed to get through to the hospital and was allowed to speak to his adjutant, the first question he asked was, 'Where's my whisky?'

'Ouch, sorry sir, it's my leg.'

'What's your leg got to do with it? Did you get a supply in, as I asked?'

'No sir, sorry, sir. I was on my way to the village and had this accident.'

'Oh, sorry and all that,' the General unbent briefly to sympathise. 'But that doesn't solve the problem. Where do I lay my hands on it?'

Algy made an effort. 'I did try to order some on the phone.'

'Yes,' the other asked eagerly. 'What happened?'

'I'm afraid they're out of stock, sir.'

'What, how long for – this is terrible.'

'I gather it's a matter of some weeks.'

'Weeks?' the General nearly yelled down the phone in his frustration. 'What am I supposed to do in the meantime?'

'I gather they have an alternative, sir.'

'What's that?'

'They couldn't promise, but they did mention they had a sustaining alternative – a healthy cordial, I believe it is called.'

But the General did not wish to hear any more. He slammed the phone down.

Concerned at his somewhat erratic behaviour, Aunt Emma consulted William on the possible causes. 'I don't know whether you have noticed it, dear, but I can't help feeling worried about your dear papa. He's behaving rather oddly lately.'

'Ah,' said William diplomatically. 'In what way?'

'When I came across him he was throwing everything out of the larder, looking for something. Do you know what that might have been?'

'I expect he was looking for something to drink.'

'Why didn't the silly man ask me. I know what it is,' she hit on a possible solution optimistically, 'he's pining for his morning cup of tea, that's what it is. I'll go and put the kettle on.'

'I think he's hoping to find something a little stronger, Aunt Emma,' suggested William tactfully. 'He's missing his usual tot.'

'You don't mean that dreadful craving for alcohol.' She almost spat the word out as if it soiled her mouth. 'I thought he'd got over that. For a man in his position, he should be showing an example. He should be doing something about the house, for instance. I don't know what Lord Beddington will say when he sees the state of it, after all this time. The paper's literally peeling off the walls in places.'

'I know, Uncle keeps on phoning me about it,' William said, aggrieved. 'He keeps threatening to come home, despite Matron. And what with this Lavinia business...' He shifted uncomfortably.

'What about it – has he told you the latest?' she asked keenly.

'Only that she's threatening legal action,' he admitted

bitterly. 'And Dad can't do anything about it because he's up to his neck... oh, I shouldn't have said that.'

'Come on, William,' she encouraged him kindly, 'you can tell me. Get it off your chest.'

And so it all came out. How he had been tricked into finding himself in bed with Lavinia after that knock-out drop and threatened with marriage and a lawsuit, when all the time he was really in love with Kate and they both wanted to get married, but couldn't afford it because both their parents were stony broke.

As the fragmented story reached its conclusion, Aunt Emma drew in a deep breath. 'Why didn't the silly man tell me all this? If I had known I could have set his mind at rest.'

William glanced up, mystified. 'But I thought you'd already left all your money to a charity?' He looked embarrassed. 'I mean, it's none of my business, of course.'

'You're quite right, William. So I was, but I can always change my mind, can't I? I know,' she said lightly, linking her arm in his, 'why don't we root your father out and put him out of his misery?'

To say General Duncan was astonished and delighted at the change of heart would be the understatement of the year. 'But this is splendid news,' he gasped. 'I can't believe it. Has William told you all about the hazards of such an undertaking?' He wanted to be quite sure, as soon as he got his breath back.

'He has.'

'And has he pointed out that the odds of finding a treasure in the bay after all this time are about the same as winning the national lottery,' he persisted, wanting her to be clear about the risks involved. 'And if it fails, I shall never be in a position to pay you back?'

'It's my money, isn't it? I think I've reached the age when I'm capable of deciding what I like with it. I vote we go ahead and find that treasure.'

He regarded her devotedly, like a well worn traveller coming unexpectedly across an oasis in the middle of the desert.

'You might lose the lot,' he warned, as a last supreme effort of self-sacrifice.

'I know, but isn't it going to be fun,' she exclaimed blithely with girlish glee. 'And think of all the benefits and jobs it's going to provide for everyone, and all the tourists it will attract. What a marvellous money spinner it will be. It will put this part of the world on the map for everyone to see. Why, I haven't been so excited about anything for years. Do let me enjoy my one last chance of a real adventure. Why don't we make an event of it and go out and celebrate?'

'Why not,' agreed the General looking suddenly cheerful at the thought. 'Which reminds me, I promised to call back an old wartime buddy of mine from the States I met in London the other day. He's only there for a few days. We've got a lot to catch up on,' he added, smacking his lips in anticipation, thinking of all the drinks he's missed in the last few days.

'Before we do anything, you'll have to tell me all about it, so we know where we are,' said Aunt Emma firmly, getting back to essentials. 'William tells me that someone is already looking for this treasure – is this true?' she demanded, ignoring the frantic signals from William to be discreet.

The General huffed and puffed indignantly. 'Some fellow who served under me at one time – an out and out Commie, if you ask me. Name of Bartlett, Len Bartlett – Kate's father,' he added reluctantly.

'Dear me, what's that got to do with it? His politics don't matter in a case like this. Surely we can come to some sort of arrangement, especially if it's Kate's father we're talking about – why, he's almost one of the family.'

'Exactly, Dad.' William joined in enthusiastically, sensing support from a new ally. 'Kate's already got a map that shows the location, so all we've got to do it to go and find it.' He looked at them both, hoping they'd agree, so that there would be no more barriers to him getting married.

Noticing her nephew's reluctance, Aunt Emma asked tactfully, 'What's the problem, Roderick dear? Is it because of Kate's father?'

Grasping at the straw, he answered gruffly, 'Can't stand the fellow – never have done.'

Coming to a decision, Aunt Emma pointed out, 'Be sensible, Roderick, don't let your pride get in the way. Try to think of it as a purely business matter, dear. All we have to do is to find an intermediary. What's wrong with asking Kate to carry out the negotiations? She seems a nice, intelligent girl. I'm sure William can testify to that, can't you dear?'

'I should say so, Aunty,' agreed William, bursting with enthusiasm. 'All she has to do is to say she's found a private benefactor who's willing to invest in the project. As Aunty says, it's only a matter of agreeing the terms.' He looked round triumphantly as if that settled the argument.

Cornered, Roderick nodded reluctantly, wishing he had his adjutant present to give his advice on the proposal. 'As long as we keep it private I suppose that's all right. If it ever got out...' He shuddered, remembering Lavinia's threats about a lawsuit.

'Well, that's all settled,' beamed his aunt. 'All we need to do now is sit down with Kate and work out what would be a fair offer. Let's make it a 50/50 deal – that should be enough for everyone concerned and make it a bumper wedding present for William and Kate.'

In William's eyes she was no longer just Aunt Emma – she was his fairy godmother.

11

OPEN TO VISITORS

To say that Len Bartlett was particularly overjoyed when he learned about the proposed terms would be a slight overstatement.

'They want 50/50?' he screamed. 'Are you mad? After all the time and money I've spent on the scheme – a measly fifty percent? I should cocoa. I wouldn't even cover my costs.'

'But Pa,' Kate pointed out patiently, 'we don't even know how much it's all going to be worth even if we do manage to find it. Be reasonable – I thought it was a good offer.'

'Call that a good offer?' ranted her father. 'I'd rather kill myself than hand it all over to that blood sucker, whoever it is.'

'What else are you going to do?' asked his daughter practically. 'The man from that loan company called around again when you were out. He was most persistent.'

'Who was it? I hope you didn't say when I'd be back,' he asked anxiously.

'He said you'd remember. Funny that, you know how peculiar some of your friends are. He had this extraordinary habit of smacking his hands together and clenching his fists as if he was shadow boxing when he was talking – I think he must have been a prize fighter at some time.'

Her father looked thoughtful. 'Hmm, I see. Did this mysterious donor of yours have anything else to offer, apart from the split?'

'Oh yes,' said Kate casually, as if as an afterthought. 'He did say he'd cover all your outstanding costs, if you agreed.'

'Did he indeed.' Seizing on the excuse of the benefactor's sex as a golden opportunity to avoid another visit from the debt collector, Len flung his arms up in the air, hiding his delight at the news and saying, 'A *man*, why didn't you say so in the first place,' as if that made all the difference. 'Now I know what you're talking about. That changes everything, now I know where I am. He did say *all* the costs didn't he? That's crucial.' He wasn't quite sure what the word meant because he'd never used such big words before, but it sounded impressive.

'Of course, Dad – does that mean you agree?' Kate threw her arms around his neck thankfully and kissed him.

When Kate phoned back later bubbling all over with excitement, news of her father's acceptance was greeted with satisfaction by Aunt Emma. 'Now we know where we are,' she declared, echoing Len Bartlett's sentiment. 'You see, Roderick, we women do have our uses after all.'

Seeing that he was expected to say something, General Duncan congratulated her hurriedly, looking over his shoulder as he did so, half fearful that Mrs Fox Cuddles might have heard their conversation.

'Right, now that's settled, I suppose we'd better put it in writing,' decided Aunt Emma briskly. I'll get in touch with my solicitor in the morning. Meanwhile, it wouldn't do any harm if you went and had a look at this exploration outfit of theirs and see what they've been up to. It needs a man to look after that side of things.'

'Of course.' General Duncan puffed out his chest importantly. 'Come, William, this is man's work.' He rubbed his chin. 'On second thoughts, I'd better change into something casual. We don't him to see my uniform or he might guess who we are.'

Arriving at the harbour, he was gratified to see a notice fixed to the nearest bollard announcing that the exploration ship named 'The Hunter' was open to visitors that very day and that a sightseeing launch was about to cast off.

'This makes it all the easier, William my boy. What a bit of luck, quick, in you go,' ordered his father, 'we might not get another chance.' As they ducked down into the boat and squashed in next to a fat lady clutching a small boy, he whispered hastily, 'Don't say who we are, if they ask. I'll think of something.'

'Ladies and gentlemen,' a voice floated down from the front, 'let me introduce myself. I am Lieutenant Krasman...'

'A good old English name,' quipped William. 'I wonder where the Captain is.'

''Probably helping himself to a nice big drink below deck, lucky devil,' muttered his father enviously.

'...and I am sure you are dying to know what we are doing in these parts...'

'Get on with it,' said William impatiently under his breath.

'You are about to witness the start of a great adventure of all tims... in leeking for goold...'stuttered the voice, lapsing into his native tongue. 'Pardone, my Engleesh is not good.'

'You can say that again.'

'Quiet, William, I can't hear, with everyone talking their heads off.'

'Sorry, Dad.' They both strained their ears, hoping to follow what was being said. During a break in the disjointed and critical remarks of the crowd around them aimed at the speaker, William whispered, 'I think he's talking about that equipment they're using... asdic or something, I think he said.'

Running out of breath, the speaker started waving them forward to see the equipment for themselves and they found themselves moving along in a queue, waiting to take their turn. 'Good thing we didn't rope in Aunt Emma,' whispered William, 'she'd be squashed in this lot.'

'I hope it's worth it,' agreed his father, beginning to wish they hadn't wasted their time, instead of making for the nearest pub, as he had hoped.

As they neared the strange looking equipment, the speaker droned on, 'As you can see, ladies and g'hentlemen this h'equipment is the latest vard in scientifeek techno... gear. It can detect the slightest movement under ze warter...'

'I doubt if it can work with all this blasted noise going on,' complained his father. 'Go on, you try it,' as they were invited to take their turn handling it, 'I can't move with this lot jamming me in.'

William took up the controls gingerly and to his surprise became quite interested in how it operated. He became so fascinated in the pictures projected of the underwater operations that he had to be prodded in the back by the man behind him in the queue before could be persuaded to give way and let his father take his turn, but found he wasn't interested.

'Tell me about it later, I've had enough of this mob,' muttered his father under his breath.

After another rambling discussion by the speaker it seemed as if he had had enough as well. 'Ladies and geentlemeen, eef everyone would be keend enough to sign the book before leefing...'

'About time, too,' sighed the General. 'A fat lot of good that was. Now, what shall I put us down as... oh, I know.' He glanced up at the name plate on the mast overhead and scribbled, "Albert Hunter". 'That should do the trick.'

He turned and was about to join the other visitors departing in the boat tied up alongside when a hand slapped him on the back heartily.

'Not going already... General Duncan, is it not?'

'That's torn it,' mumbled William.

'I beg your pardon?' spluttered his father. 'I'm afraid you're mistaking me for someone else. My name is... um, Desmond... Hunter.'

'Ho-ho, that's a good one.' The other winked and dug him in the ribs. 'I know you – your face has been in the local papers. You are the gentleman staying at Beddington Hall, yes? You are here, how you say... incognito?'

'Quick, scarper, Dad,' advised William, about to do the same.

Lost for words, his father was about to try to bluff his way out when the stranger held up a hand jovially at the hunted expression on his face. 'My friend, you do not have to pretend with me. Allow me to introduce myself. I am Captain Borshak. I am in charge of this vessel.'

'How do you do,' answered the General politely. 'Now if you'll excuse me...'

'But you are going so soon? I cannot permit that. You are too distinguished a gentleman to refuse my hospitality.'

The General hesitated for a moment at the thought and licked his lips. 'Hospitality, did you say?'

'But of course, my limited resources, such as they are, await your approval.'

'Dad, don't forget...'

The General swallowed and disregarding his warning obediently followed the captain down to his cabin, as if in the middle of a blissful dream.

'Oh, what's the use,' argued William to himself. 'Too late now. I'd better see that he doesn't get into any mischief.'

'You see.' The captain waved his hand at a row of bottles lined up on the sideboard, as he settled himself. 'What can I offer you? Ze brandy, gin, whisky – a poor collection I'm afraid but it is all I have. I hope you will forgive me.'

General Duncan moistened his lips and spoke in an awed whisper. 'Have you a Scotch whisky, by any chance?'

'Of course, my friend, be my guest.' He poured a generous helping and passed it over to his visitor.

The General swallowed it gratefully and held the glass out hopefully again.

'Another, but why not. Help yourself,' said the captain amiably and passed over the whole bottle before holding up his glass in a toast. 'Good luck, my friend. Being a soldier of fortune like myself, you don't need to stand on ceremony on my ship. We stand shoulder to shoulder – up the republic.'

'Dad, don't you think...' But he was too late. His father was making whinnying noises like someone who had just been released after a life sentence on a remote island and waved him aside. Disregarding his host's political leaning, he accepted the offer with both hands and poured himself another liberal helping of whisky.

In a desperate attempt to divert his father's attention before he sank beyond recall, William appealed directly to their host.

'You were saying about the object of the exploration, Captain erm... Borrowshack...'

'Borshak.'

'Of course, forgive me. You were saying...'

The captain stretched himself and took up a more comfortable position, waving his glass. 'You English, so impatient to get to ze point, are we not, eh? Let me tell you,' he helped himself to a glass of wine that looked as if had just been uncorked for the first time in fifty years and reached out a lazy arm to pour another, 'I hear that some idiot is paying for all this now, so here goes – cheers, as you say, down ze hatch.'

'Cheers,' they both responded automatically, reacting to the unexpected disclosure.

'Yes, where was I?' The captain's speech was getting a little slurred by now and he started to reminisce. 'If I were to tell you about all the struggles I've been through to get where I am today you would never believe me... never.' He stared at them, becoming more and more belligerent as he waved his arms around dramatically.

The General finished another glass with a shaky hand and looked around for a refill. 'Whass that you say?'

William interrupted gamely, battling on. 'The captain was just telling us all about the diving operation, weren't you, Captain?' He shot an agonised glance at their host in vain. It was like waking the dead.

'Ow!' The captain swayed as he attempted to get to his feet and accidentally kicked the table in passing to demonstrate his point, nursing his foot in surprise. 'Who put that there?'

'The sunken treasure – where is it?' William persisted as a last resort.

That woke him up. The captain looked around owlishly. 'Ah, that would be telling.'

'Is it a secret?'

'It depends on how much it's worth.' The other leered cunningly.

'But you're being paid to find out,' reminded William indignantly.

'Ah, that's what they think. If they want to know where it is, they'll have to cough up.'

William blinked at his remark and looked around for support, but his father was already half asleep. The whole thing was beginning to look very odd, he decided.

It was time they got back and talked it over before they went any further. He glanced at his watch and nudged his father. 'I think it's time we were off, Dad. Aunt Emma will be getting worried.'

But the captain wasn't ready to lose their company yet and made it clear in no uncertain terms. 'What's the matter – d'you think I'm bluffing? See for yourself, my friend.' He searched in his desk drawer and after a lot of digging pulled out a map.

'There, that'll show you,' he crowed triumphantly, jabbing at the figures.

'But that's...' William stopped and nearly gave himself away, recognising it as the identical one that Kate had shown them.

'You think I don't know what you're up to?' the captain accused, waving it in their faces as he swayed on his unsteady feet. 'Coming here pretending to be tourists – I know what you're after. You want to steal it, don't you. Well, I'm not going to let you.'

'Wha-at's he saying?' asked the General foolishly, lifting his head, aware that he had missed something. 'Something about the map?'

'Don't worry about it now, Dad,' William warned, anxious to get away after all they had heard. He turned apologetically to their host. 'I really think it's time we went. Thank you so much for your hos...'

The captain barred their way menacingly. 'You don't think you're going to get away that easily, do you? You think I'm a pushover, don't you. Let me tell you, I've dealt with your sort before.' His mask slipped. 'You're nothing but bloated plutocrats, the whole pack of you. When I was fighting in the jungle with my back to the wall, who do you suppose came to my rescue? No, not you lot – my comrades, that's who. Fascists, that's what you are.' He stumbled over the word furiously. 'Oppressors of the poor, that's your game.'

'Who's he talking about, William? Sounds a load of rubbish.'

'Lean on me, Dad. I really think we ought to leave.'

'Wait a minute.' The General swayed on his feet. 'Who's he calling fascists? Anyone would think he was a blasted Commie.'

The captain drew himself up to his full height. 'What was that you called me?'

The General tried to look dignified. 'A Commie – short for communist. You've heard the phrase, haven't you?'

'That's what I am.' The other beat his breast proudly. 'A man of the people – what of it?'

The General was stunned. 'Do you mean to say we've been harbouring a wretched Commie all this time under false colours? I have you know our family is British to the core. We'll have nothing to do with damn Commies. It's a bally insult.'

Having got that off his chest, his eyes rolled and he collapsed on the floor at their feet.

Managing with difficulty to gather his father up and help him off the trawler and making for the nearest bench seat available – provided by the Council along the quayside to encourage tourists – William took a deep breath and wondered what to do next, while the General began to snore gently by his side. Realising that he daren't get his father back in his present condition and face the wrath of Aunt Emma, he cast a desperate glance around and caught sight of the magic words, "Turkish Bath" on the nearest signpost. Wishing he had Algy to help him, he hoisted his father up again with difficulty.

'Come on, Dad, make an effort. We're nearly there.'

'Wh-at? Just having a little sleep.'

'Haven't got time for that, later on. Up we come, we're going to have a nice soak.'

'Soak, did you say?' His father's eyes lit up. Sounds like a good idea.'

'No, not that kind of soak – come on, easy does it.'

. . .

After the impact of a cold shower and an invigorating towelling down afterwards, the General cast his mind back with an effort to the conversation they had had with the captain on board the ship they'd just left.

'What was it that confounded man called me – a bloated plutocrat? Damn cheek, I call it.'

'He didn't mean it, Dad. He'd just had too many,' soothed William, trying to calm him down, hoping to get him into a reasonably fit condition before returning.

'Wait a minute,' exploded his father suddenly. 'I remember it now, he called me – a fascist! You heard him, he's nothing but a Commie, just like that Bartlett fellow. "Up the revolution" indeed. I've a good mind to go back and get him to repeat it, the swine.'

'Dad, forget it – you can't start anything now,' implored William, seeing his plans for getting married going up in smoke. 'If you do that he'll go and complain to Kate's father and you won't be able to keep it a secret any longer.'

'No, there is that, I suppose,' his father admitted reluctantly.

'And bang goes our chance of sharing in that treasure, especially after Aunt Emma has offered to pay for the costs,' William reminded him bluntly. 'We'll just have to live with it.'

'I imagine it's too late now to get hold of another captain,' pursued the General wistfully.

'Not at this stage,' said William firmly, 'it's too late. Besides, he's too well known around here now to find anyone else. You might get some awkward questions. I know he's a queer character, but they all seem to like him.'

'What's that you're saying about our Probsey?' called out a passing attendant.

'We wouldn't do without him. He's only been here five minutes and he's brought new life to the folks around here, ain't he, Joe?'

His friend Joe spat in agreement. 'Never said a truer word,

Tom. Why I mind the times when half the folks round here hadn't got two pennies to rub together like, it was that bad.'

'Now everything's different,' enthused Tom. 'It's a different kettle of fish altogether. People are queuing up all hours of the day to hear about that there treasure they've been going on about. It's gone and transformed the place – not the same anymore, thank God.' He joined his friend spitting happily at a passing gull.

Seeing the way the conversation was turning, the General interrupted hastily, 'It's good to hear everything's going along smoothly.'

His rather lukewarm acceptance caught the other's attention. 'Why, have you heard anything different, mister?'

'No, no, I was just checking,' was the hasty response. 'Now if you'll excuse us, I think we must be getting along.' The General lumbered to his feet.

Taking his cue, William echoed his father. 'You're right, Dad, I'd no idea what the time was.' He waved his hand in farewell. 'So pleased to hear the place is back on its feet again. We must look you up again sometime. Bye.'

'Crikey, that was a close thing, Dad,' he mouthed. 'I thought we'd never get away.'

'It's just a question of how you get on with people,' puffed his father pompously, as they made their way up from the quay. 'I always say it's better to speak your mind.'

'Quite,' said William diplomatically, shutting his mind to their earlier encounter. 'No, I think it's better this way,' he added, steering his father away from the direction of the pub.

As they reached the main road he thought back over their recent conversation with the captain and voiced his concern. 'I hope he doesn't spill the beans to Kate's father about our visit.'

'I don't believe he will, if he's got any sense,' puffed his father. 'I gather from what he was saying that he's all out for number one. He probably thinks he can do a deal with us on

the side. He's that sort of man, a thoroughly nasty character –
still what d'you expect from a Commie.'

'Don't let's mention it to Aunt Emma,' urged William. 'We
don't want to put her off the whole idea.' He let slip without
thinking, 'She might even agree to pay off some of your Mess
bills at this rate.'

His father remarked drily, 'That idea had occurred to me.'
Then as the full significance of his remark penetrated at the
thought of her predictable reaction to the size of his drinking
problem, and the threat of facing a bleak future without his
nightly tot of whisky, he clutched William's arm frantically.
'Don't dream of saying a word to Aunt Emma about it – the very
thought of it haunts me every time I think about it.'

William swallowed. 'I was just joking. If she finds out how
much you owe, you'll never hear the last of it.'

'Exactly.' The General shuddered. 'Let's hope that never
happens.'

12

GETTING INTO DEEP WATERS

I n the event, it all passed off relatively easily, much to their relief. Although questioned very closely on the visit, the General's stout assurance that everything went splendidly seemed to satisfy Aunt Emma for the moment.

'There you are,' she remarked complacently. 'I told you it needed a man to deal with the situation, didn't I?'

'You certainly did,' replied the General buoyantly, uplifted and immensely relieved at her acceptance of what had undoubtedly been a fiasco.

'So how's it all going?' Has that captain of yours got any results yet?'

'Oh my word,' bluffed the General, 'it's coming along *splendidly*,' finding comfort in the word. 'William seemed fascinated about it all, didn't you, my boy?' He cast a meaningful look at his son for support.

'Yes, funnily enough, I did,' agreed William, surprised at the discovery. 'That asdic equipment we saw was certainly worth a visit. I wouldn't mind having another go at that – I wonder how it works?'

'Never mind about that,' interrupted his father hurriedly,

glancing at the clock and seeing they were getting into deep water. 'I'm sure Aunt Emma doesn't want to know every little detail. Besides, I've got an appointment with Mac this evening – I mean Major-General McKinrick, my American opposite number – in the Embassy, you know,' he ad-libbed hastily for his aunt's benefit. 'He's over here to boost Anglo-American relations.'

'I didn't know they needed boosting,' sniffed his aunt. 'I can't argue with that. While you're off gallivanting up to London, I suppose I'd better get that letter off to Len Bartlett before he changes his mind. What are you going to do, William?'

'Me? Oh, I think I'll have a word with Kate and also Uncle Henry,' he said, catching sight of all the messages on his phone and eyeing his father significantly. 'Just to let them know what's happening.'

'Yes, you do that, William,' boomed his father, relieved. 'We mustn't let them get the wrong ideas, eh? My word, is that the time – I must be off.'

Left alone after his father had gone, William wasted no more time before getting in touch with Kate.

After bringing her up to date with the situation as tactfully as he could, he asked anxiously, 'You haven't told your dad about us... I mean about Aunt Emma backing his scheme?'

'Good heavens, no. What do you take me for – do you want it all ruined?'

'No, of course not.' He breathed out thankfully.

'Right then, tell me all about it. How's it all going? I mean the exploration?'

'Fine,' he said quickly, changing the conversation. 'D'you still love me?'

'What a silly question.' She relented. 'You don't have to ask me that. I wonder what that Lavinia is up to,' she mused. 'I mean, now your Aunt's frightened her mother off.'

'I shouldn't worry, she's probably got her eye on someone else by now.' He dismissed her fears as groundless. 'Let's talk about our own wedding plans. Once we get that fixed she can't worry us anymore.'

Despite his confident talk, the subject of their conversation had no intention of giving up her efforts to salvage something out of her wrecked plans. Harping on the subject to her mother on the phone, Lavinia seethed with fury. 'If he thinks he's getting away with it, he's got another think coming,' she declared with a determined toss of her head.

Although her mother was unable to see the gesture, she felt that her daughter had made her point so forcibly that she quailed for a moment. 'Now promise me, darling, you won't do anything silly now, will you.'

'Don't worry, Mumsie. Between you and me, I've been in touch with Chuck, that old boyfriend of mine and he's given me the name of a top lawyer.'

'Not too expensive, is he, darling?' her mother asked anxiously.

'It'll be worth it, Ma – he's the goods, I tell you.'

'Before we go that far, darling,' she said hastily, 'I've got a feeling we need to do a little more ferreting around and find out what that Aunt Emma of his is up to. I'd just got him where I wanted him over coughing up the necessary loolah when she practically ordered me out of the house – said she was looking after him.'

'Wow – d'you think she's changed her will again?'

'I don't know, but I intend to find out. I was planning to invite him to the next parish meeting to see what gives, but he gave some excuse about seeing an old wartime buddy of his up in Town. While he's away I thought you and I could do some sniffing around.'

'What d'you have in mind, Ma?'

'I don't know, but that wretched Len Bartlett is looking mighty pleased with himself over that pet marina scheme of his. It all sounds rather fishy to me.'

'Count me in, Ma, I'm free this weekend. What d'you have in mind?'

'I think we might pay a call on that boat of his in the harbour. I hear they give conducted tours. You never know, it might give us some clues. I'll leave it to you to dress for the part, if you know what I mean.'

'I get you, Ma. I'll put on my best outfit – that should loosen some tongues.'

Unaware of the danger threatening, William felt he could now make the most of his precious time with Kate before his father returned with any more of his drinking problems.

'I know,' he suggested, struck by a sudden idea, 'why don't we get away from it all and have a picnic somewhere to talk things over.' Before he could elaborate on his proposal his phone bleeped at the crucial moment and he snatched at it, irritated.

'Yes, who's that? Oh, it's you, Matron. Is – is everything all right? Oh, it's Uncle. What's he done now... tried to what... escape down the drainpipe? You want me to come and calm him down?' He sighed resignedly. 'Okay. I'll be right over... yes, promise. Thank you.'

He sank back on the bench where they were sitting and rubbed his face despondently. 'I wonder what he's been getting up to now. I suppose I'd better go.' He disentangled himself reluctantly and started heaving himself up. 'About that picnic,' he reminded her.

'What a lovely idea,' she enthused, 'I know just the place – down by the old mill – but go and see your uncle first. I'll pack up some things while I'm waiting. Make it this afternoon. See you, darling. Leave it to me.'

After a prolonged kissing session that left him more frustrated than ever, he left for the hospital, half wishing his uncle had fallen off the drainpipe and made a good job of it.

What made it worse, he found his uncle tucked up in bed looking remarkably fresh after his escapade as if it were an every-day occurrence.

'What have you been up to, Uncle,' he asked, without much hope of getting a satisfactory answer.

'You've got to do something, William.' His uncle looked at him feverishly, as if he were about to repeat his escape attempt at any moment. 'I can't stand it here any longer. All the time I'm lying here I keep thinking of the state the Hall is in with all those men pulling the place to pieces. You told me you were going to keep in touch. And Edith keeps on at me so...'

'I know, Uncle,' soothed William. 'But so much has been happening since I saw you last.' He hurriedly announced Aunt Emma's offer to back Len Bartlett's exploration project to look for the buried treasure and laid stress on Aunt Emma's promise to repair any damage to the Hall.

At the mention of repairs, Henry Beddington glanced up hopefully, clutching at the life-line for one glorious moment, thinking they had at last found a saviour, then sank back moodily as he recalled the old superstitions attached to the sunken treasure story. 'Oh, that old wives' tale – she must be mad, bless her. Who persuaded her to do that, for heaven's sake.'

'Well, Dad's all for it,' urged William, reinforcing the argument. 'And we all are,' he added, trying to sound convincing.

'In that case,' answered the patient, giving up. 'You're all mad, the whole lot of you. Thank you for telling me, William. I'll pass on the riveting news to Edith. I can't wait to hear what she's going to say about it.' He shut his eyes, dismissing the latest news of little account. 'Now, if you don't mind, I'd better try and catch up on some shut-eye to give me strength to tell your aunt.'

Patting his uncle's hand, William took the opportunity to escape, fortified by the prospect of sharing a picnic with his beloved.

When they arrived at the place Kate had in mind the weather and the scenery seemed to be conspiring together to show the location at its best. Nearby, a group of swans sailed past majestically on the Mill pond, a solitary badger had climbed out to see for himself who the intruders were, and the birds in the trees were lining up to greet them with a chorus of welcome. Even a sleepy caterpillar poked his head up to see what all the fuss was about.

'Darling, what a heavenly spot,' breathed Kate, filling her lungs with a fresh breeze that was beginning to dance through the surrounding heather, casting a magical spell around them. 'This is my favourite place – I can even see our back garden from here so we won't have far to go when we've finished, and you can come and say hello to Dad. That reminds me, I promised to take back some fresh flowers, ours have practically wilted away from all this weather. Don't I deserve a kiss for discovering it?'

William gladly wasted no more time and got down to it, setting the seal on her happiness. Up to that moment, he had not allowed himself to think about what she meant to him, amidst the mounting problems that had clamoured for his attention, and the sudden contact of her warm body close to his aroused an urgent longing that set his nerve endings on fire. Scarcely knowing what he was doing, he helped her set out the contents of the basket and arranged the cutlery with shaking hands, trying hard not to look at her while he was doing it, in case he gave himself away.

'Mmmm, that was delicious.' Kate lay back contentedly on the grass afterwards, feeling the cool breeze play over her. At the sight of her lovely limbs stretched out, he was about to gather her up in his arms when she sat up with a cry of vexation. 'What am I thinking of? I promised Dad I'd bring back some fresh flowers for his party tonight – he's invited some special guests hoping to find some backers for his treasure hunt. Now don't get up, darling,' as William reached out for her hungrily, 'I know exactly where they are, just the other side of that little brook.'

She eluded his grasp and darted away, waving an empty bag, leaving him to follow on behind. 'Look, there they are,' she cried a little later, pushing his hand away excitedly. Getting ready to jump across, she glanced behind as she was talking, lost her balance and fell in, pulling William after her.

Later on, after she searched for some dry clothes for him upstairs in her father's bedroom, she found him peeling off his shirt in the bathroom, trying to mop himself up with a towel. 'Oh, William, what do you look like?'

He turned. At the sight of her standing there in her clinging dress, it was too much. 'Oh Kate, darling,' he cried hoarsely. 'I can't stand it any longer, let's go to bed.'

'Go to bed?' she gasped. 'What are you talking about?' All she wanted to do was to get out of her soaking wet clothes and jump into a scalding hot bath.

'I mean... Bed...Beddington Hall,' he said hurriedly. 'Forgive me, darling, I don't know what I'm saying.'

'That's not funny,' she cried. 'What kind of girl do you think I am?'

Coming to his senses, William was full of remorse. 'I'm sorry, I got carried away. Please forgive me, Kate. Please.'

Drawing herself up, Kate refused to be mollified and some of her earlier doubts began to resurface and gather strength. Unable to hide her feelings any longer, she burst out passionately, 'Carried away, indeed. If I'd have known you were going to behave like this, I would never have come.' She drew in a deep breath with a sob. 'And to think I trusted you after all those things you said about Lavinia.'

'But Kate, you don't know how much I've missed you. You mean everything to me.'

'So it seems,' she replied indignantly, grabbing hold of a dressing gown and putting it on with shaking hands. 'If your conduct is anything to go by, I think that Lavinia has had a lucky escape – I'm not surprised she's bringing a case against you.'

'I thought you cared for me,' he uttered wretchedly. 'Does that mean it's all over between us?'

'Yes, it most certainly does,' she decided, fighting back her tears. 'I never want to see you again.' She threw the clothes at him as a final gesture and stumbled away.

After dabbling himself in a futile sort of way, William collected up his wet things and set out for home with a heavy heart. He was about to head for the stairs and a hot bath before retiring to his bed for some sort of comfort when he received a hearty slap on the back and a familiar voice greeted him.

'I say, what-ho.'

He turned his head dully, wanting desperately to be left alone to hug his grief in peace. 'Oh, it's you.'

'I say, that's no way to greet the old wounded hero, what? Sorry about the stick and all that. The doc at the hospital seemed to think I needed one for a bit because of that leg injury of mine. I felt like giving him a biff with it – take more than a silly old spill on the bike to put me out of the running.'

Ignoring the banter, William refused to be drawn. 'I'm sorry about your leg. Dad's up in London looking up an old wartime friend of his and Aunt Emma's around somewhere, And... oh hell,' he said, letting his feelings out in a rush. 'I wish I was dead.'

'What's up, old sport, not girlfriend trouble again. I thought I heard your aunt had given Lavinia's mother her marching orders.'

'Oh, it's not that,' answered his friend dispiritedly.' It's Kate – she's given me the brush-off.'

'What, not Kate the golden girl. I thought you two were going steady, all ready to rush up the aisle together. What's happened?'

Gathering his scattered wits, William proceeded to relate for the second time that day about recent events, culminating with news about their joint bid for buried treasure and their fruitless visit to the search vessel and their encounter with the left-wing captain until his mind grew dizzy over the complications involved.

'But that doesn't explain why Kate has given you the brush-off,' said Algy patiently. 'Why the glum expression?'

William grew red with embarrassment. 'After all that business with Dad and his drinking and the treasure hunt, I got so carried away at the picnic we had that... um... I sort of... forgot myself.'

'Why you wicked old lad, I didn't know you had it in you.' Algy regarded him in a new light. 'So all that caveman stuff didn't work, eh?'

'You can say that again,' said William gloomily. 'She says she doesn't want anything more to do with me.'

'This needs thinking about.' Algy looked thoughtful. 'Have you tried the old forgiveness gambit?'

'Yes, she said she thought Lavinia had a lucky escape and she wasn't surprised she's bringing a case against me.'

'Ouch, that's laying it on a bit thick. Hmm, I wonder if we need to look at this in a different light. Supposing we accidentally let slip to Kate's father that your dad is the silent partner, for instance?'

'What? Dad would never hear the last of it. Talk sense.'

Algy carried on regardless. 'Ah, but don't you see? In that case, Kate's dad would do anything he could to keep the arrangement going smoothly whatever happens. He would do his best to persuade Kate to think again about her attitude.'

William could not agree, much as he would like to. 'You don't know Kate. Once she gets an idea in her head, nothing will shift it. Look at the trouble we had in persuading her that I was tricked into bed with Lavinia after she gave me that knock-out drop.'

'What about thinking up some spiffing scheme for saving her pet dog then?'

'She hasn't got one.'

'I know, what about inviting old Len Bartlett to look over this exploration boat of yours and push him over the side and dive in and rescue him. That would go over big.'

'Kate told me he is an excellent swimmer – he'd probably end up rescuing me.'

Algy was stumped for a moment, then brightened up. 'You could always tell her your heart is broken and all that rot and threaten to join the jolly old Foreign Legion.'

'I've already tried that – she said, "Ha."'

'You don't think it was more like "Ha, I'm too upset to answer"?'

'No, more like a "Ha, ha", showing her contempt.'

Algy scratched his head. 'I can see I shall have to think this jolly old problem of yours over and see if I can come up with any more wheezes. Meanwhile, I'd better touch base with this Aunt Emma of yours. We've got to keep someone happy on the home front.'

'Yes, you do that,' replied William, sunk in the deepest gloom. 'I'll probably go and shoot myself.'

Putting on a jaunty air he was far from feeling, Algy set off in search of Aunt Emma. He found her mulling over a secret problem of her own. Putting aside her own puzzles that had been vexing her, she bustled forward, full of concern at the sight of Algy's stick.

'You poor man, whatever have you been doing with yourself. Are you all right?'

'I'm fine,' he reassured her. 'And how's life treating you – everything shipshape, as they say?'

'It's funny you should ask me that. Young William's been going around like a sick cow – I don't know what's got into him. He won't tell me, the silly boy.'

Algy coughed diplomatically. 'I believe he's going through the normal give and take of boyhood romance. Nothing too serious,' *I hope*, he added to himself.

'Oh, thank heavens for that. I'd hate to have his father come home and have to deal with another family crisis.'

'Other than that, everything hunky-dory, what?'

'Well yes and no.' Aunt Emma hesitated. 'I've just come across something rather mysterious. I'd be glad to have your opinion on it, seeing that you know Roderick better than I do.'

'Anything I can do to help?'

For an answer, Aunt Emma led him to a cupboard in the General's bedroom and fetching out a stool climbed up and rummaged around on top. With a sigh of satisfaction she pulled out a bundle of receipts that Algy had come to know so well. It was the General's Mess bills.

'How did you come across these?' asked Algy swallowing, taken aback at the sight.

'I decided to do a bit of dusting and thought I'd better tidy his room up while he was out. We haven't been able to get anyone to do this sort of thing properly – I can't ask Jarvis, he's got enough to do as it is.'

'Quite,' agreed Algy, trying to feverishly think up a plausible excuse for the incriminating evidence in her hands.

'Anyway, let's get back to this mystery. What do you think it means? They seem to add up to rather a lot.'

'Ah, well you see they're er... my... um... Mess Bills,' he gulped, improvising on the spur of the moment. 'I don't know what they're doing there. I wondered what had happened to them.'

'*Your* Mess Bills?' she repeated in amazement. 'But they're astronomical. How can you hope to pay them back on your salary?'

'I've come to an arrangement with the Mess Sergeant,' he managed glibly. 'You'd be surprised what they're willing to do these days.'

Taking a second look, she said sharply, 'Then why are they signed 'Roderick Duncan', that can't be right, surely. Why isn't it signed in your name?'

'Ah, I thought you'd ask me that,' he said, stalling for time. 'I didn't have my pen on me at the time and he very kindly signed it for me.'

'You seem to have been in a habit of losing your pen rather a lot by all accounts, haven't you?' she enquired disbelievingly.

'Yes, I do rather,' he agreed weakly, running out of excuses.

'Well, I'm not satisfied,' she said placing the receipts in her handbag and closing it with a snap. 'I shall have words with Roderick about this. If he thinks he's getting back to those nasty habits of his, drinking behind my back, he's got another think coming.'

13

OLD PALS' REUNION

B lissfully unaware of the storm clouds gathering behind him, the General set off for his meeting with his old American wartime pal, feeling almost in a schoolboy mood again. As soon as he reached the reception in the hallowed entrance of the Regency Palace he made himself known and asked for his old friend.

'Major General McKinrick did you say?' repeated the prim young lady with a pronounced accent, in keeping with her surroundings. 'If you will kindly take a seat, I will let the gentleman know you are hearah.'

The General sat down gratefully, happy to take the weight of his feet.

As he relaxed lost in thought, memories of the past reminded him of the great times he and his old friend had enjoyed together and he couldn't wait to see him again. So when the lift opened and his buddy emerged he was somewhat disconcerted to see him being helped out by an attendant, complete with luggage, ready for departure.

'Bugsby,' he cried, 'don't say you're going, just as I get here.'

His friend advanced, hand outstretched, profuse in his

apologies. 'Gee, glad you could make it, Rodders, you've caught me just in time. See here, there was I all set up to paint the town red when you arrived, when dang me I got this summons to report back to HQ right away – would you believe it?'

Fighting back his disappointment, the General was full of sympathy. 'What rotten luck, I was so looking forward to it. Never mind, we'll have to fix another time. Let me know when you're free.'

'I sure will, it's not often I get the chance to get away when duty calls – just when you've gone to all this trouble to get here. I don't know off the top of my head when that'll be – you know what our bosses are like. They like to know where you are all the time. I can't even down a drink without them breathing down my neck.'

Thinking of his own situation under the strict observation of Aunt Emma, Roderick agreed whole heartedly with a sigh.

Struck by a sudden thought, his friend came up with a bright idea. 'Say, why don't you come back with me to the base for a few days instead and talk over old times – we sure have a lot to catch up on, and the drinks would be on the house, I'll see to that.'

It was the mention of drinks that made up his mind. Without a second thought he beamed his acceptance, then hesitated, thinking about the problems he'd left behind. 'I'd love to, only my aunt has decided to join us unexpectedly and my son William's expecting me back.'

His host waved his hands, dismissing any worries he might have. 'Bring 'em along – the more the merrier.'

'I'm not sure my aunt would appreciate your welcome,' he said hurriedly, aghast at the thought she would be watching him with eagle eyes. 'But I'm sure William would like the opportunity, he's mad keen on flying.'

'Good, that's settled. Get him to throw some things in a bag and I'll send my driver down to collect him and anyone else you want to bring along.'

Losing no time, the General phoned William, thinking it would give him an excuse to stay away longer and make the most of his friend's generous offer.

Overhearing his father's summons, Algy made frantic signals to have a word and proceeded to break the news about Aunt Emma's discovery of his mess bills.

As the words sank home, the General nearly dropped the phone in a panic, mentally cursing himself for leaving the incriminating evidence behind. Breathing heavily, he managed, 'You'd better come along as well and we'll have a meeting about it,' he said, glancing behind and hoping nobody overheard. Dabbing his forehead again he added, 'A car will be along to pick both of you up. I'll leave you to explain something to Aunt Emma.' Overcome at the thought of his aunt brandishing the bills in his face and demanding an explanation, he tottered off to seek a reviving drink to soothe his shattered nerves.

'That'll give him something to think about,' remarked Algy thoughtfully as he replaced the receiver.

'I expect he's off to drown his sorrows, lucky devil,' brooded William. 'I feel like joining him.'

'Cheer up, old lad. It can't be as bad as all that. Young Kate's probably missing you just as much, if you did but know.' Changing the conversation at the lack of response, he enthused, 'Sounds a generous old bird, this chum of your dad, inviting us down as well. You never know, you might even get some free flying lessons out of it.'

'D'you think that's likely?' asked William doubtfully. 'I've only been up once or twice before – they're sure to ask.'

'Bound to be someone dying to take you up – you'll get on

like a house on fire, trust me.' Algy slapped him on the back. 'At least you won't hear anything about Lavinia while you're there.'

His forecast proved correct in one respect. When their host was reminded about William's flying ambitions when they were introduced, he waved all objections aside. 'Gee, a man after my own heart. I've got just the fella who'll be glad to take you up. Chuck?' He waved a beckoning hand. 'Where are you? Come and meet our visitors.'

A chunky looking officer strolled up and nodded casually. 'Hi!'

His Commanding Officer pulled him forward and beamed. 'William, you don't mind me calling you that, do you? We don't stand for any formality around here, not like you Brits,' he joked. 'Eh, Rodders?'

General Duncan smiled sheepishly, wondering when they were going to get another drink. 'Er, quite so, Bugsby.'

'Only kidding, Rodders. Say, William, if you wanna get some air time, here's the very man for you. Have a word with Chuck Malone, our latest recruit who's just joined us – he's in charge of our training session, just the guy you need to meet.'

Shaking off his depression with an effort, William put on a welcoming smile and found himself gripped in a beefy handshake.

'Hi, there, William, or can I call you Willie?'

'Most people call me, Bill,' he offered apologetically.

'Bill, then. Say, why don't we find ourselves a drink and get to know each other?'

'That sounds a great idea,' echoed their host, much to General Duncan's relief.

'This call for a celebration, eh, Rodders? I tell you what. Chuck, why don't you take William and Algy down to your quarters to freshen up after their journey while Rodders and I catch up on things? Meet you in the bar in about,' he consulted his watch, 'half an hour, when we'll grab a bite to eat?'

'Okay by me, sir,' agreed Chuck readily. 'This way, folks.'

'I say, what a splendid place you've got here, Chuck,' enthused Algy. 'Plane spotters' paradise, what? Just what you've been looking for, William.'

Taking his cue, William expressed his thanks awkwardly. 'It's very good of you to spare the time to teach me – I've hardly had the time to think about it lately, much as I'd like to, what with one thing and another.'

'Think nothing of it, Bill,' said Chuck as he changed into a more comfortable jacket. 'It'll help take my mind off my other problems.'

Catching sight of his moody face in the mirror as he washed his hands, Algy said jokingly, 'Don't say you've got girlfriend trouble as well.'

'It's not so much the girl.' Chuck clenched his hands, nearly snapping his comb as he smoothed his hair back. 'It's that slimy, treacherous rat she's got involved with.'

'There you are, William – and you thought you had a problem.' Turning to Chuck he explained, 'Don't worry, his is only a temporary tiff.' And to his friend, 'Cheer up, she'll come round, you see if I'm right.'

'She told me she never wanted to see me again,' mourned William. 'Bang goes any wedding hopes I had.'

'Don't talk to me about weddings,' ground out Chuck. 'There was my girl, the only one I've ever loved, and before I know it she gets hitched to some toffee nosed creep who gets cold feet at the last minute and backs out just when the date's been fixed and everything.'

'I say, that's not on,' murmured Algy in sympathy. 'Sounds a bit of a swine, what?'

'You've said it, buster. If only I knew who he was. Just let me get my hands on him, that's all I ask. I'd tear him into a thousand or more pieces.'

'How many?' asked Algy jokingly, trying to ease the situation.

'Let's say he'd wish he'd never been born.'

'Hm,' reflected Algy. 'Thank your lucky stars you don't have that little problem, William.'

'It's not the same. It wasn't me who got cold feet,' said William despondently. 'I'd give anything to get Kate back.'

'You've said a mouthful, Bill,' agreed Chuck. 'Gee whiz, I'd give a million dollars to get just one little kiss from Lavinia.'

'Have you got a million dollars, Chuck?' managed Algy, doing his best to bridge the deathly hush that followed.

'I will do when my old man strikes that dogonned oil well he keeps on promising me.'

'Wait a minute,' wavered William. 'Did you say, La-Lavinia?'

'Yea, a peach of a name. I get spooked out every time I think of her.'

He shook himself wistfully. 'Why, have you heard of her, where you come from?'

'Me?' stuttered William. 'What makes you think that?'

'I guess it's a might unusual sorta name. And her ma's a big noise on the local Council I hear – goes by the name of Fox Cuddles, can you beat that?'

'The name seems familiar,' said William faintly. 'What do you think, Algy?' He flung a desperate look of appeal at his friend.

But Algy was already looking at his watch for inspiration and interrupted hastily. 'I say, chaps, I don't want to rush you, but shouldn't we be joining the others? I don't know about you, but I'm getting a bit peckish.' Tossing an imaginary glass up to his lips he added meaningly to William who was still looking stunned at the news, 'I should think your dad needs bringing up to date – on what the time is, if nothing else. Knowing him, I expect he's had more than his fair share by now. I'm sure he'll be interested in all your news.'

'Ye-es, I think he certainly will be,' was all William could manage.

Agreeing, Chuck hoisted himself up. 'You've said a mouthful, I expect they both are well on the way by now. Come on, let's see what they're up to.'

But one look at his father told William he wasn't going to get any help in that direction. Disregarding an eloquent warning gesture from Algy, General Duncan couldn't wait to bring them up to date with a solution to his own problems. 'Don't give me that "need to know" nonsense Frobisher, Bugsby here has come up with a brilliant idea about that little, ahem, trouble with my Mess bills. Tell 'em, Bugsby.'

'Nothing to it, Rodders, my old friend. Gee, when I think of all the wars we've been through together over the years and the holes he's got me out of, why this is the least I can do for him. The answer's dead simple.'

'Oh, and what's that – are we entitled to know?' enquired Algy quickly, anxious to steer the subject into safer waters before the dreaded mention of Lavinia cropped up again.

'Why, we'll say there're *my* Mess bills, not Rodder's, don't you see?'

'But-but, how d'you make that out?'

'Don't you get it? I'll spell it out. My old buddy, Rodders here, invited me down to his place as soon as he got there, and being his guest he signed all the mess bills I'd run up, on my behalf.'

Algy coughed. 'Was any, um, figure mentioned?'

'Who cares?' Bugsby laughed, slapping his old friend on the back. 'I'll just add it onto mine.'

'If I may be permitted to ask, how can you, um, manage that?' asked Algy cautiously.

'Why we're spending a small fortune on celebrating the anniversary of that little old dust up we had in the last war. Nobody'll notice the difference. That reminds me – I expect Chuck here will do with a little help doing his usual fly past routine, dropping balloons and things for the locals – all part of our neighbourly gesture of good will. What about it, young William – you willing to give a hand?'

'Of course he will,' decided his father, raising his glass. 'I'll drink to that. Here's to our Anglo-American alliance.'

They all raised their glasses.

'Besides,' hiccupped the General, casting all caution aside, 'by the time we've found that treasure of ours, I'll be able to run up as many Mess bills as I like.'

'Gee, what treasure's that, Rodders? Don't say you've been holding out on us?'

'Ahem', coughed Algy, 'it may be a little premature at this stage, sir. It's not exactly official yet.'

'Nonsense, Frobisher, you're just an old stick in the mud. Why shouldn't I tell my old friend?' He waved his hand expansively, nearly losing his balance in the process.

Algy coughed. 'If you remember, sir, the agreement has yet to be signed.'

'What of it?' The General became truculent. 'If that idiot Len what's his name knows what's good for him he'll sign on the dotted line.' He held out his glass. 'Oh, thanks. Bugsby.' He raised his glass for another toast to emphasise his words, flinging out his hands in an extravagant gesture, swaying as he did so. 'Here's to our treasure hunt. You haven't heard the half of it yet. You're never going to believe the rest of it, but when I tell you...' The effort was too much for him, and he overbalanced and collapsed at their feet.

'I say,' said Algy, mopping his forehead at their near escape.

'I believe he's out for the count. Sorry about this, chaps – if someone could give me a hand?'

'Of course,' William volunteered anxiously, relieved that they had been spared any further damaging revelations. 'Let me help.'

'No, I insist. We'll take care of this, it's not the first time this has happened with our guests. Chuck, do you mind – looks like my old friend Rodders needs an extra hand.'

'Sure, leave it to me.' Thrusting the others aside, Chuck hoisted the General up on his shoulders with ease and nodded to Algy and William. 'Lead the way, guys. All he needs is a bit of shut-eye to sleep it off. He'll be as right as rain in the morning.'

However, when morning came the General had not only forgotten about their conversation, he didn't even seem to remember who he was or what he was doing there.

He raised a bleary eye and fumbled with his duvet, trying to thrust it aside. 'Where're my clothes, dammit? What am I doing here? Can't lie here all day when there's battles to be won. Don't trust that Castro. Well, don't just stand there – who the devil are you?' He focussed his eyes at Algy as if it was all his fault.

'I'm your adjutant, Lt Frobisher, sir. I say, are you all right?'

'Never heard of you. What are you ringing that blasted bell for?'

'Just seeing if the doc's around to check you over, after last night, sir.'

'Last night? What happened last night?'

'If you remember, sir, you had a little, um, accident.'

'Nonsense, never felt fitter, and who are you?' He glared at the sight of William, coming to see how he was.

'It's me, Dad. How are you feeling after last night?'

'Rubbish, never seen you before, where are my clothes?

Can't stay here arguing with you lot. Got more important things to do.'

'Of course, sir,' said Algy soothingly. 'You just wait here a minute while I get the steward and rustle up some of your things.' He winked at William. 'While I'm doing that, my friend here will look after you. Can we get you something to drink?'

'Well, hurry up – make it a strong one. Haven't got time to sit around here while the Commies are waiting for the chance to take over, right?'

'No, of course not, Father... I mean, sir,' he gulped. 'Ah, here's Algy now.'

'This is just what you need,' encouraged Algy, holding out a glass. 'It'll put fresh life in you.'

The General eyed it distrustfully. 'Rum sort of drink – doesn't look like whisky to me.'

It's stronger than a whisky,' promised Algy. 'Knock it back and we'll get you fit enough to fight all those Commies of yours single-handed. Scout's honour.' He crossed his fingers behind his back.

'Oh, all right.' The General shut his eyes and tossed it back. The next minute Algy picked the glass out of his unresisting fingers and laid him back on the bed.

He regarded the slumbering patient thoughtfully. 'I don't know about you, William, but I think the sooner we get him away from all this booze before he lets the cat out of the bag, the better.'

'I'm with you there.' William swallowed. 'If we stay here any longer there's no telling what he might come out with.'

'At least that little knock-out drop will take care of him for the time being,' said Algy, satisfied. 'Mind you, I'm not sure how we explain it all when we do get back.'

'What came over him?' William marvelled. 'It sounds as if he'd lost his memory – he didn't even seem to know who I was.'

'I can only think he must have got a spot of concussion

when he fell over last night. All he needs now is a lot of tender loving care – I'm sure we can rely on Aunt Emma for that.' Algy smiled ruefully. 'At least we won't hear anything more about those darn Mess bills. She'll be so concerned with nursing him better, I expect she'll have forgotten all about them when she sees the state he's in. That reminds me, William, how do you feel about staying on and giving Chuck a hand with his fly-past celebrations?'

His friend heaved a sigh. 'I suppose I'll have to go through with it, since Dad's already promised – but I'm not exactly looking forward to it, now we know all about Chuck and Lavinia.'

Algy patted him encouragingly on the back. 'If you can manage it, you'll be doing us all a great job. Come to think about it,' he added struck by a sudden thought, 'it's almost a blessing in disguise. You'll be able to keep us posted on all the latest about that action threat of Lavinia's. Don't you see, now's your chance to bolster his hopes in that direction and make him think he's on to a sure fire winner. Play your cards right and it could get us out of a nasty hole. We're relying on you, old sport...' He broke off at a knock on the door. 'That must be our driver now.' He raised his voice, 'If you could give me a hand, oh, can you manage Okay? Splendid.'

As he turned to follow the procession out, he whispered. 'And when you see our host I should tell him not to worry about his offer about those Mess bills – he'd never survive the shock if he knew what he'd let himself in for.'

14

INFATUATED WITH THE GEL

When he woke the next morning, William made a mental note to follow up Algy's advice after a spot of breakfast, but when he got down to thinking about it he became more worried about the actual sleuthing angle and how he should go about it, bearing in mind his new friend's temperamental behaviour regarding a certain subject. To help him concentrate on the problem, he put his feet up again to assist his thoughts and the next thing he knew half the day had gone and he was still none the wiser.

Remembering his promises, William finally plucked up courage and sought Chuck out. Following the revelations about his host's relationship with Lavinia, he was aware that he was treading on thin ice and was not looking forward to the prospect. However, if there was even a remote chance that it would help patch up things with Kate, he was all for it.

After checking his friend's quarters, he finally traced him to the hangar where he noticed a giant pair of boots sticking out from under the fuselage of what looked like a relic of past battles fought and won. He bent down and greeted his rival. 'Hi, Chuck, anything I can do to help?'

A tray rolled out and Chuck emerged, wiping his face with a cloth. 'Appreciate the thought, Bill. Nope, just giving the Dak a once-over ready for the flypast. Say, I could do with a break. Why don't we mosey over to the canteen and grab ourselves a can of something?'

Seeing that he was in an amiable mood, William readily agreed and fell in beside him, trying to keep up with the massive strides the other made.

Over a drink or two, his host slapped his glass down with appreciation. 'That's better. Now, what about it? Are you ready for off?'

'You mean the flypast?' William couldn't believe it was that time already.

'Nope, your lessons, chump. Still interested, are you?'

'Yes *please.*' He couldn't hide the sudden feeling of excitement about the tempting offer but thought he'd better be honest about it. 'I've only been up once or twice before getting here and that was ages ago.'

'Don't worry, you'll soon get the hang of it. Come over to the hanger and we'll sort you out.'

As soon as they arrived, he fished around in the store. 'Here, grab hold of one of these and try it for size while I go and wheel the old trainer out.'

'Thanks.' Catching hold of the flying suit thrust at him, William clambered into it, zipping it up as he did so.

'Oh, and you'll need the old crash helmet to go with it,' Chuck added with a grin.

Feeling more like a robot, William walked up and down getting used to the unfamiliar garb, while Chuck disappeared into a nearby hanger and re-emerged at the controls of a sturdy looking fixed wing trainer, proceeding to taxi around in a half circle, ready for take-off.

Pushing up his goggles, he pointed at the cockpit seat behind him and shouted above the noise of the engine, 'Grab a seat, Bill, oh, and don't forget to plug in your intercom while you're at it, otherwise you won't hear a doggoned thing.'

William stepped up on the wing gingerly and, sliding the canopy back, climbed into the seat and fastened his seat belt, waving his hand in acknowledgement as he did so.

Almost immediately, Chuck's voice came through, vibrating in his ears. 'Can you hear me, Bill, okay?'

'Yes,' answered William, holding his ear piece away with a grin, 'loud and strong.'

'Okay, we'll do a few simple circuits to let you get the feel of it and when you're ready I'll pass it over to you to try. Okay?'

William swallowed. 'I hear you.'

'Good. Don't forget to let me know if you get stuck or anything.'

'Don't worry, I'll soon tell you.'

'Okay, here we go...'

Much to his surprise, William soon got over his initial panic and began to revel in the pure enjoyment of the experience, feeling completely safe in the hands of his instructor. He found himself treasuring every moment as soon as he was allowed to take over the controls, and lost all idea of time as he first circled then tried a tentative descent before Chuck took over again at each landing approach.

'There, how was that?' Chuck slid the canopy back finally and beamed at him. 'Ready for a spot of grub now?'

Much to his surprise, William felt hungry after all the excitement of completing his first successful solo. 'A boiled egg would go down a treat,' he admitted cautiously, half expecting his friend to have his mind fixed on a more lavish meal, going by the size of him.

'No worries – I think we can manage that.' He patted his stomach. 'Me, I'm on a diet. Got to get into shape for my love.

Seems to think I could lose a stone or two – I ask you. Some women are never satisfied.' After finally managing to peel off his bulky flying suit he admitted bashfully. 'Mind you, I'd do anything for that doll. Tell you what, you go ahead and bag a table while I get rid of this clobber.'

William did as he was bid, only to find the canteen packed out. He was about to give up when he was hailed by a familiar figure seated at one of the tables.

'Come and join me, Bill, I've just finished anyway.'

Catching sight of his host, William became flustered. 'I don't want to disturb you, sir, I was just waiting for Chuck.'

'The more the merrier. Come on, sit yourself down. Knowing Chuck, he's probably waylaid by something or other, he's always like that. Now, what'll you have – a full house, as you limeys call it?'

'No, an egg would do me fine.'

His host waved the modest request aside. 'Nonsense, you can't survive on just one egg – waiter!'

An attendant materialised by his side. 'Yes, sir?'

'Fetch half a dozen boiled eggs for our guest here while he decides what to have.'

'Yes, sir – coming up.'

'Now, enough of this 'sir' business, call me Bugsby like your dad does. Tell me, how've you been getting on, son – is Chuck looking after you?'

Pretending not to hear the bit about adopting a more familiar nickname with such a senior authority, despite being an old friend of his father's, William answered the latter appeal. 'Yes, it's been brilliant. I've picked up all sorts of tips.' Hastily correcting himself, not wanting it to sound too boastful, and aware that he should give Chuck more credit, he enthused, 'Of course, to a beginner like myself I expected it to be difficult at first and thought it would take some time to get used to it. But when you think we were only up there for an hour or so, with

Chuck showing me the ropes, I feel as if I've been flying for ages – he makes it look so easy.'

'Good. So you still feel up to giving him a hand with our flypast tomorrow?'

'Gosh, is it tomorrow already – I forgot about that. Yes, I'd love to help in any way I can.'

'That's great. I feel I can leave you in no better hands then.' He glanced around to make sure there was nobody in earshot. 'Between you and me, Bill, I owe my life to the young rascal. True,' he explained further at William's look of astonishment. 'What people don't realise is that Chuck has a multitude of other talents. You've heard his old man is hoping to strike oil down in Texas, haven't you?'

William nodded, not wanting to reveal the full extent of his knowledge in case it all came out about Lavinia.

'Well, Chuck firmly believes he's going to strike a gusher any day now – but that's by the way. I've never told you about his old man, Abe, have I?' He fiddled with his knife and fork reminiscently. 'I tell you, he's the only man who ever got me inside a Church Hall to listen to one of his sermons on the subject. Anyway, it all came about when we had to knock down an old building on site in the early days to make way for a new hanger and we were pushed for time. Dang me if Chuck didn't come up with the answer on the spot. It seemed that all we had to do was to ring his old man and get him to airlift a crate of explosive charges over on the next flight, so of course I was all for it. No red tape involved. Just the job – spot on, as you might say. It went ahead as we planned and he got stuck in and did a marvellous job.' He paused ruefully. 'What he didn't tell me was that he intended to let off another lot of charges to make sure of things.'

'What happened?' William's throat dried up in anticipation.

'Only that yours truly, dumbhead, thought it was all cut and dried after the first one went off and couldn't wait to have a look at it for myself and *whoom,* I nearly went up with it when the second one hit us. Luckily, Chuck saw me and pulled me out of the way, just in time. So you see, I've always had a soft spot for our young superman – even if he gets involved with all kinds of whacky girlfriends on occasions. And if you've ever seen the latest, you'll know what I mean. If his old man does strike lucky with a gusher this time, she'll be after him like a shot, you mark my words.'

William was about to ask him more when his host looked up with a satisfied bark of welcome. 'Oh good, here's your egg order. I'll leave you to get stuck in. Feel free to follow it up with anything that catches your fancy – it's on the house.'

Left on his own, William was about to decide which egg to start on when a heavy hand descended on the table with such violence that half of the eggs shot up out of their egg cups and splattered over the table cloth in all directions, leaving a trail of sticky egg yolk behind them.

'What the...?' Groping for his napkin in a futile attempt to mop up the mess, William turned to see his friend, a thunderous expression on his face, venting his fury by kicking the table, adding a few more broken eggshells to the shambles in the process.

'You may well ask! You don't know who I've just been speaking to?'

'No, how could I?' Then trying to diffuse the situation he added, 'Why don't you sit down and tell me all about it?' He waved helplessly at the waiter hovering in the background and was relieved to see him start to mop up the mess. A thought suddenly occurred. 'Something wrong with the trainer – is it something I've done?'

Chuck sat down heavily, so overwrought that he could hardly get the words out.

'No, nothing like that.' Then, as he managed to master his

emotions, he spat the words out. 'You'll never guess who that was on the phone.'

Trying to calm his friend down, William did his best to soothe him.

'So it was nothing to do with the plane – a bit of unwelcome news from home?'

Disregarding his attempts to lighten the situation, Chuck dropped his first bombshell. 'That was Mrs Muriel Fox Cuddles,' he shook his head irritably, 'of course, you wouldn't know her.' His voice took on a note of worship. 'She's Lavinia's mother.'

William managed. 'Really. Both in good health, I trust?'

It proved too much for his friend. He ground his teeth. 'No, they are *not*.'

Then he pulled himself together. 'They thought they'd go and check up on what was happening with that pathetic treasure hunt operation down at the docks... a perfectly innocent enquiry.'

'Naturally, and...?'

'And d'you know what that Captain whatever his name is...'

'Borshak?' William said without thinking.

Chuck broke off and eyed him suspiciously. 'How come you know his name?'

'Oh,' William floundered. 'I thought everyone knew that. He's got a terrible reputation, I hear.'

'Yes, something like that. Anyway, after inviting them below he got them both so tight they could hardly stand.' He saw William nod in sympathy at the recollection and questioned sharply. 'I suppose you've heard all about that as well?'

'Er, yes, um news gets around, you know.'

'Not content with that, do you know what that hound had the infernal cheek to do?'

'Charged her for the drinks?' offered William at random, doing his best to diffuse the situation.

'No, you idiot. The rat put his arm around her and... *pinched* her!'

'Pinched her – handbag?'

'No, you dumbbell – her bottom. You wait until I'll get hold of him.'

Overcoming a sudden overwhelming urge to laugh, William hastily rearranged his features to express a suitable look of disgusted horror and tut-tutted in sympathy.

'And that's not all. She was too upset to speak to me about it, but from what her mother told me he also made a pass at her as well.'

'Golly, he must have been blind drunk,' said William without thinking.

'Well, by the time I've finished with him, he'll need it,' was the grim reply.

After a pause, William managed to ask, fearing the worst, 'What did you have in mind?'

'I'll think of something – something that will shut him up for good.' Then remembering his duty as host with an effort. 'Don't forget the flypast is tomorrow.'

'Looking forward to it. It's been such a long day, full of... unusual events. I think I'll have an early night, if you don't mind.'

'Go ahead,' Chuck agreed absently, in a thoughtful way as if he was turning something over in his mind. 'That reminds me, I think I'll just check on things down in the old stores hanger while I'm at it – to see if I've locked everything up all right.'

William was struck by a sudden uneasy feeling. Wasn't the hanger he was talking about the place where they did all that rebuilding work – where Bugsby nearly got blown up and where there might still be some charges left over that he could get his hands on?

As soon as he got to the safety of his own quarters he shut the door behind him and sat looking at the telephone, his head full of whirling indecision, wondering what he should do. Then, looking at his watch, he made up his mind and picked up the receiver. 'Hello, switchboard, I wonder if you could put me through to an outside line? The number, oh yes, I have it here somewhere.' He fished an old letter out of his pocket, giving his uncle's home number. 'Yes, here it is...'

'Hello, who's that... Algy – thank God it's you. Listen, is there anyone about? No, well there's been a frightful bust up at this end. You'll never guess what's happened.' He swallowed and brought his friend up to date with everything that had taken place that day and ended feverishly with, 'Hello, have you got all that about the explosives – are you still there. So what the hell are we going to do?'

'Yes, I'm here. I'm just taking it all in – give me a moment.' Aware that the events that had occurred placed William in a difficult position, Algy began tactfully outlining several alternative courses of action. Thinking aloud, he suggested diffidently, 'I suppose the only right and proper way to go about it would be to pass the whole thing over to the C.O and let him deal with it – after all, it's his responsibility.'

There was an immediate howl of protest. 'We can't do that. Chuck's my friend – I can't do that to him. I know he's an idiot at times, particularly over Lavinia, but it would finish him off. Old Bugsby would have to clap him in irons.'

'I thought you said Chuck had saved his life at some point. Surely that would weigh in his favour.'

'I wouldn't bet on it. He would be bound to stick by the rules. We can't take that chance.'

Algy adopted a reasonable attitude. 'He didn't strike me as the sort of chap to go that far.'

'You don't know Chuck. He's a hell of a nice guy but when he gets worked up the sparks begin to fly. You should have seen him in the canteen – he nearly blew his top and threatened blue murder.'

'But you don't know if Chuck has got any charges available to carry out that kind of threat.'

'No, that's true.' William debated to himself. 'But I don't like the way he talked about going to lock up the hanger where he kept them.'

'The only way we can find out is for you to go and search all the likely places.'

'Blast, I've left it too late now. I'll have to leave it until morning.'

'You do that.' Algy said, relieved to know they were given some breathing space. 'Just as well, he'd probably see you following him around. Now you know what to look for, it should be easier to find them in the morning.'

'Okay,' agreed William reluctantly. 'I'll call you as soon as I hear anything.'

'Yes, don't hesitate, whatever the time – I'll make sure you get put through. Don't forget, you've got that flypast to do in the morning. Meanwhile, in case he does try anything silly, I'll get onto the powers to be to persuade that wretched Borshak to move his blasted boat away from the dock out to sea, so he can't get any more supplies of booze delivered whenever he likes. Golly, that should cause a rumpus. I don't know what the General and Len Bartlett are going to do when they hear about it,' he said, knowing full well as he said it how his nibs would react at the loss, once he understood what it was all about.

Left to himself, William was left in no doubt in his own mind about the threat Chuck posed, if he really meant what he said and intended to follow it through. The only snag was, how could he prove it? He glanced out of the window and saw that it was already getting dark, making it almost impossible to find anyone without being challenged. But it was no good, he had to find out, otherwise he'd stay awake all night. Glancing around, he snatched up a pair of rubber sneakers and slipped them on before grabbing a torch. Tiptoeing to the door, he opened it a crack and listened, ignoring his thumping heart beats.

All was quiet. Then he heard a click of a latch being closed in the near distance and a brief flicker of a torch. He made his way as quietly as he dared towards the sounds of movement, catching a quick glimpse of Chuck as he was closing the latch on the front of the recently rebuilt hanger where Bugsby said they held all their stores and – William caught his breath – where they kept any of the explosives left over. Hardly able to think straight while chasing away the anxious fears that were buzzing around inside his head, he drew near as he could without being spotted.

He could just make out the outline of Chuck who appeared to be dragging something along behind him on a trolley as he approached the hanger where the two fighters were housed.

Heaving up the shutters, his friend turned on the lights and William was able to see the objects more closely – two slim packages, the contents hidden from view. William could only hazard a guess as to what they might contain and the thought sobered him instantly.

Before he could think what to do, Chuck stepped back and began closing it all up again, making the decision for him. With a quiet smile of satisfaction, his friend dusted his hands and strode back to his billet, leaving William with the problem still unresolved. Were they really the deadly explosive charges he'd been told about, that his friend was cheerfully heaving around with blithe unconcern, or could they simply be an innocent load of fireworks, ready for the anticipated firework display?

He remained there undecided, then finally gave up and followed suit. It would have to wait until tomorrow, when he might have a better chance to find out the truth.

· · ·

Meanwhile, Algy had his own problems to sort out. After pondering on the potential repercussions that might occur, he replaced the receiver and muttered, 'What a bugger.' Slipping on a jacket as if to emphasize the gravity of the situation, he paused for a moment, deciding on his next step. Who should it be – Aunt Emma or the General? On reflection, it was no good alerting the General although he had made his views well known in no uncertain terms about 'that blasted Commie', as he called the captain. Much as he detested the man, he would hate the thought of losing all that readily available booze. Algy shook his head. Anyway, in his present condition the General was in no fit state to offer any sensible advice after that bout of concussion, believing as he did that he was back in the age of the Castro regime. So it would have to be Aunt Emma.

Accepting the alternative with some misgiving, he started looking for her in the sitting room, then remembered that she had decided to retire early with a migraine. Should he leave until tomorrow? No, better get it over with – what he had to tell her would be enough to give her a bad enough headache, as it was. Better do it gradually, otherwise she might get so worked up about it she could even decide to stop funding the treasure hunt altogether, and where would that leave them? He shuddered. Bang would go their chances of ever paying off those darn Mess bills, for sure.

Heaving a sigh, he mounted the stairs to her room. The last thought that crossed his mind as he tapped on her door was that he must never let on about that visit of theirs to the boat – Aunt Emma would never let them hear the last of it.

Much to his surprise, when he broke the news about the treatment Lavinia and her mother had undergone in the hands of Captain Borshak, Aunt Emma seemed to have a job keeping a straight face. First she began to giggle and immediately clapped a hand over her mouth, then forgetting herself she gave way and rocked with unrestrained laughter at the thought of the indignity they had suffered. Finally, she mopped her eyes.

'Most unseemly,' she apologised at last. 'What a brute. Still, serve her right for being such a nosy parker. Fancy threatening to bring a breach of promise case against poor William. Indeed, I've never heard of such a thing. And where did he get all that drink from, I ask myself – who's paying for it?'

'I imagine he was charging it up on his expenses,' said Algy, trying to change the subject.

'It's a good thing he didn't have the nerve to offer any to Roderick when he went there... he didn't, did he?' A shadow of suspicion crossed her face for a moment.

'Good heavens, I should think not indeed,' said Algy quickly. 'I wasn't there on that occasion, but I'm sure he would have told us otherwise.'

'Well, I hope for his sake he didn't, otherwise I would have given him a piece of my mind,' she said severely. Then another thought occurred to her. 'Do you mean to tell me I've been paying for all these disgusting drinking orgies as part of our treasure expenses?'

'I suppose it depends how far back you agreed to lend a hand, as it were. If I may suggest a possible solution...'

'Go on.' She looked stumped. 'What's the answer?'

'I suppose, if for instance, he was given instructions to move his boat out into the bay, well away from his present moorings, that would make it safer, and,' he added cunningly, 'he would find it difficult to maintain his existing supplies.'

'What an excellent idea – we'll do it right away. That will stop his little game. Well done, Algy. See to it, will you. You'll have to say it's on behalf of the General, as nobody officially knows I'm involved yet. Make it sound feasible, like you've heard there's a storm coming up and there's danger to shipping, something like that.'

'With respect, I fear it would have to come more directly

from Mr Bartlett who has chartered the vessel, otherwise I fear it might not prove acceptable.'

'Hmm, that means I'll have to get in touch with him. I don't fancy that, he's such a difficult man to deal with. I know, what about that daughter of his... Kate, isn't it? Could you get hold of her and explain it. I'm sure she'll understand.'

'If I might remind you, m'am, there appears to be some sort of friction between her and master William at the moment.'

'Oh yes, I'd forgotten, there's always *something* with that family. Well, I can't help that. Their feelings with one another must take second place at the moment, this is too important to argue about. Do your best and explain the position to her and let me know what you come up with.'

'I'll do my best, m'am.'

'I'm sure you will. Another thing. Can't William do anything to restrain that boyfriend of Lavinia's – Chuck or someone? We don't want him to get stirred up about it on her behalf.'

'I fancy master William is already aware of the potential problems that might arise, m'am. In fact, he's already promised to ring me if there are any further developments.'

'I hope you're right, Algy. You never know what these young men can get up to if he's infatuated with the gel.'

15

BARMY'S THE WORD

It was the fly buzzing on the window behind the curtain that
woke him up.

For a moment, William forgot where he was. Then it all
came back to him.

Chuck and those blasted explosives – how was he going to
talk him out of it?

As if in answer to his dilemma, the man himself rapped on
the door and poked his head round the corner. 'Gee, aren't you
up yet? D'you know what the time is?'

Shaking his head with an effort, William apologised. 'Sorry,
I must have overslept. Am I late?'

'Well, not all that late, I guess – it's only ten past nine. But
we've got to get our skates on. According to the latest weather
forecast it's going to cloud over later on so they've decided to
hold the flypast this morning instead, which means,' he
checked his watch, 'we need to take off in just under an hour
before the big-wigs turn up to make the announcements. Are
you still able to give a hand?'

'Of course.' William threw off the bedclothes and sat up.
'Give me five minutes and I'll be with you.'

'Great, I'll tell Cook to rustle up a quick bite to eat. See you in the canteen.'

'Right.' As he quickly washed and dressed, William noticed his friend's voice sounded unusually stressed with an undercurrent of excitement, quite unlike his normally cheerful and relaxed manner. But he had no time to think any more about it in the rush to get ready.

'We should be okay,' said Chuck gulping down his coffee. 'Urgh, tastes like dishwater.'

In his present half awake state, William helped himself to a mug and savoured the aroma. 'Blissful,' he announced gratefully. 'That's put fresh life into me.'

'You're going to need it,' broke in his friend. 'Not the flypast stuff, that's dead easy, it's what comes after.' Covering up his slip, he added hastily, 'No probs, we've got the old Dak laid on – it should be ready by now. All you have to do is to stand in the doorway, all strapped up so you don't fall out, and when I give the signal you heave them out, one by one, and wait for the cheers from the crowds.'

Noting the puzzled look, he explained, 'Don't worry about the fireworks. They're all fitted with timers and a fuse, so you don't have to do a thing. We'll do a few practice runs first, so you'll see what I mean. Any questions?'

Not daring to ask about the two slim packages, William asked bluntly, hoping to evoke a response, 'So what do we do after that?'

Refusing to be drawn, Chuck pushed his chair back. 'Heck, it's up to you. I've got some unfinished business to attend to. But I guess you'll be wanting to ring up your folks and find out how your dad's getting on and making plans for going home. Ready?' Without waiting for a reply, he stood up impatiently, anxious to get on.

Hoping to calm his friend down, William readily agreed,

following him out onto the tarmac and climbing into a flying suit offered by one of the ground crew.

The business of connecting him up to the restraining straps in the open doorway on the plane took a little longer before Chuck was completely satisfied. Then he stepped back for a final inspection, catching his foot on a box behind him.

'Ouch. Dammit, that hurt.'

Twisting his head with difficulty, William looked over his shoulder and caught sight of the object responsible and recognised it immediately. It was the tail end of one of the boxes he'd seen in the stores hanger. 'That doesn't look like fireworks,' he insisted. 'How did that get there?'

'Oh, must have been one of the fitters, got it mixed up somehow,' said Chuck casually. 'Not to worry, I'll sort it out afterwards.' He dangled his foot experimentally. 'What is more important, I think I've injured my foot, blast it.'

'You should have it seen to,' urged William hopefully, looking for an excuse to postpone the exercise.

'Nix,' snapped his friend irritably. 'We haven't got time for that – I'll see the medic later. Let's get on with it.' He hobbled a few steps and caught his breath, cursing, before carrying on unsteadily into the cockpit. 'I'll – I'll be okay once we've started.'

What followed appeared to William to take on some kind of nightmare quality.

He sensed the aircraft staggering slightly on take-off, but after a few practice runs things seemed to settle down to near normal, apart from a few muffled grunts from the cockpit end. After a signal from the assembled gathering below, Chuck's voice crackled over the intercom, 'Okay, that's us – hang on... here we go...'

On cue, William fed a stream of fireworks out at intervals, one after another, bursting into a galaxy of colours, followed by waves of rockets going off at regular intervals, to the delighted appreciation of the waiting crowd below, until there were only two mysterious packages left, lurking in the background.

'That's it – all gone,' he reported finally.

'Jesus, about time too. I'm knackered,' a plaintive voice floated back from the cockpit. 'It's no good – I'll have to get this damn foot of mine fixed before I do anything else.'

William sent up a prayer of relief at the news. 'I could do with a visit to the loo while you're at it,' he fibbed, using it as an excuse, wondering to himself how quickly he could get to the nearest phone and speak to Algy. Luckily, he found one close to the toilets so he was able to get through with the minimum of fuss and delay.

'Listen, Algy, I haven't got long,' he said urgently, keeping an eye open for Chuck. 'We've just this minute finished the flypast and I've got a lot to tell you so please listen and don't interrupt.'

'I know,' came the reassuring reply. 'We've been watching it on the local news. What's happened?'

William nervously explained, trying to keep his voice steady. 'I was right, after all. He took some packages out of that stores hanger after I spoke to you... you know, the one where he kept those leftover explosives I was telling you about,' he cast a quick glance behind, 'and discovered he'd loaded them into the back of the Dak before we took off.'

'You sure about that – they're still there?'

'Yes, they're the same ones, I'm sure.'

'For heaven's sake! Where's Chuck?'

'He injured his foot on one of the boxes and he's seeing the doctor.'

'What's he planning to do?'

Unable to keep the anxiety out of his voice William said, 'He was going on about seeing to some unfinished business after the flypass was finished.'

The response was immediate. 'Well now's your chance. Get

hold of old Bugsby and stop the flight. There's no alternative. Do it *now!*'

As William wavered, his friend lost his patience. 'You don't realise. It's not only that. When he heard about the drinking going on and all the bills flooding in, Len Bartlett did his nut and ordered Borshak to leave the harbour and he had the cheek to refuse. So they've had to call the police in. Don't you understand? They're a sitting duck in the harbour. Every second counts if they're going to survive.'

William heaved a sigh. 'Okay, I'll ask one of the fitters.' He put the phone down reluctantly and stepped outside, accosting the first person he came across. 'Excuse me, how do I get in touch with Major General McKinrick, can you tell me?'

The fitter smiled doubtfully. 'You could try his secretary, sir.' Then confidentially, 'I doubt if you could get hold of him right now, he's seeing off all the VIPs after the flypast.'

'Thanks,' William acknowledged, feeling at a loss, his mind torn between loyalty to his friend and the dreaded alternative. Before he could decide what to do next, the decision was made for him.

'That's all done. Ready to go?' Chuck was standing there waiting, leaning heavily on a crutch, with one foot heavily bandaged up.

'You're not proposing to go up after that?' The whole idea seemed preposterous.

'Why not? I've still got two hands.'

'But you're mad.' William tried to think of a compelling reason against it. 'It's not safe – you might crash.' Casting caution aside, he demanded desperately. 'Why is it so urgent. What do you hope to do?'

Chuck jabbed him with his stick. 'It's a surprise for someone. I don't *hope* to do anything – I'm damned well set on it – now are you with me, or not?' Seeing his hesitation, Chuck waved him aside. 'I never thought you'd turn down a chance to help a buddy. Suit yourself, I'll manage on my own.'

'Wait.' Faced with the prospect of his friend determined to carry out his threatened mission and possibly killing himself in the process, William hesitated no longer in the hope that he could somehow prevent it happening. 'Okay. What do you want me to do?'

Chuck clapped him on the back awkwardly. 'Great, I'll explain as we go along. Help me up into the old crate and grab a seat.'

As time passed, and frustrated at the lack of news, Algy put in a call to the airbase. What he heard left him so concerned that he felt he could not keep quiet about his fears for his young friend any longer. It was time to seek wider counsel.

Knocking discreetly at Aunt Emma's door, he entered as he was bidden and without wasting any time laid the problem before her, not without some trepidation.

To his immense relief, the prospect of a threatened air attack did not upset her unduly. She was more concerned about William.

'That poor boy, what on earth can he be expected to do?' She got up off the bed briskly. 'This calls for a family council. We must see what the others have to say. They're all downstairs by now. I spoke to Kate earlier – she's bringing her dad over. Such a nice girl. If only she could patch it up with William.' She sighed and pondered. 'It's no good expecting anything from his father in his present state, we'll just have to see what that Len Bartlett has to come up with, if anything. He made a right old mess of getting that Borshak creature to move his boat somewhere safe and all he did was to upset the local bobbies when they're trying to do their duty. Just because he's on the Council, he thinks everyone's got to agree to his slightest wishes. Ah well, I think I can hear someone stirring. Let's go down and find out.'

The scene that greeted them was not unexpected as they were soon to realise. The General was already at odds with Len Bartlett, despite Kate's efforts to change the conversation.

'It's all your fault, Duncan, for sticking your nose into it in the first place. We were doing very nicely before you butted in.'

Still lost in a completely different time zone, the General replied heatedly. 'Very nicely, I like that. You were stony broke, on your uppers. If it hadn't been for me you'd be in queer street where you belong, along with your friend Castro.'

'Now then, Dad,' intervened Kate, trying to calm things down, 'don't take any notice. He doesn't know what he's saying, he's not been at all well.'

But her father wouldn't listen. 'Not well? I like that, he's round the bend in my opinion, in cuckoo land.'

'At least he kindly offered to invest in your treasure hunt, Dad, remember? After you'd put all your savings into it.'

'A fat lot of good that did. It's already cost me a fortune after he bribed my captain to indulge in all those drinking orgies.'

'I like that,' yelled the General, stung with fury. 'He was the one who invited us in the first place and tried to get us all stoned.'

'And who was it who invited all his son's old girlfriends along to cook up a diabolical scheme to get the police on him. Answer that one.'

'That was nothing to do with me,' answered the General with dignity. 'I understand your Captain Borshak behaved in a disgusting way, forcing his unwanted attention on the two ladies concerned.'

'I don't believe a word of it,' defended Len Bartlett hotly. 'They were so tight, nobody could believe a word they were saying.'

'Well, it's in the hands of the police now,' commented the

General drily. 'I put my trust in that fine body of men to do their duty.'

'While you two are arguing,' interrupted Aunt Emma abruptly, 'you'll be interested to know that the young lady's ex-boyfriend is at this moment on his way with a plane load of explosives to take it out on your Captain Borshak for the way he has treated his guests.'

The news was received with incredulity and slackening jaws. 'He's – what?' gasped Len Bartlett. 'You can't be serious.'

'Ask Mr. Frobisher here,' she invited. 'He'll be able to bring you up to date with the situation.'

'Is this true?' appealed Len Bartlett hoarsely. 'It can't be, you must be joking.'

Algy stepped forward and nodded in sympathy. 'I'm afraid it's quite true. The last time I spoke to William...'

Kate straightened up, alert at the mention. 'He's not involved, is he? I thought he was just staying on for flying lessons.'

'He was,' agreed Algy. 'But his instructor, an American pilot by the name of Chuck Malone, turned out to be a devoted ex-boyfriend of Lavinia Fox Cuddles – who you all know – and was so worked up at the treatment handed out to Lavinia and her mother that, according to William, he's managed to find some old explosives left over from his father's oil well in Texas and is on his way to seek some sort of revenge.'

In the blank astonishment that greeted his announcement, Kate was the first to recover. 'What has William got to do with it?' she asked fearfully.

'As I was saying, the last time I spoke to him I urged him to report his findings to the Station Commander and he agreed, but reluctantly, because of the close friendship that has developed between the two of them.'

'So what the hell happened,' demanded her father,

speaking on behalf of the others who appeared to be struck dumb by the announcement.

Algy turned courteously in his direction. 'Master William omitted to tell me, sir. After making further enquiries, I was informed that the Station Commander was unavailable and I gather William was persuaded to accompany Mr Malone in the hope of,' he lapsed into schoolboy jargon, 'ahem, putting a spanner in the works, so to speak.'

'But that's dreadful,' gasped Kate. 'D'you mean to say that poor lamb is at the mercy of that monster?'

'Nonsense, my boy will know how to look after himself.' The General came out of his coma after mishearing the tail end of the conversation. 'We Duncans come from fighting stock. Besides,' he assured them confidently, 'no harm will come to the crew on that boat of theirs – I have it on good authority they were all taken off for questioning half an hour ago.'

Len Bartlett sat up, outraged. 'What about my boat – it's completely at their mercy now. It's costing me a small fortune to pay for running that outfit, and all you can do is to stand there and see it all going up in smoke!'

'A good thing too,' sneered the General. 'What a squalid little affair. I hope that Commie Captain of yours gets all he deserves. And he had the cheek to call me a fascist. To think I got persuaded to back that pathetic venture of yours – what a ghastly mistake that would have been,' conveniently forgetting that his aunt had come to his rescue and bailed him out.

'Well, you *are* a fascist, everyone knows that' accused Len pugnaciously. 'A great big fat one, always strutting up and down, taking it out on the rest of us. Another little Hitler. The men used to give a two-finger salute when they saw you coming.'

The General heaved himself to his feet and threw off his jacket. 'Come and show me then, you nasty little Commie rat. If you think I'd let my son have you as a father-in-law you've got another think coming.'

His old enemy squared up and advanced threateningly. 'You must be out of your mind. Allow my Kate to marry your William when he's about to bomb hell out of my ship?' He drew his fist back. 'Take that.'

Suddenly, a small defiant shape jumped up between them and thrust them apart in desperation. For an instant, Algy could have sworn she gave him a brief, conspiratorial wink before clasping her tummy and staggering forward dramatically.

'While you two are arguing, William is up there risking his life to save your necks, doing everything he can to make this place safe for our baby!' she entreated, taking a quick peep to see how her announcement was going down.

The hot words died on their lips and all thoughts of their feud vanished from their minds as they turned to Kate, mouths agape.

'Don't you understand?' she added with as much conviction as she could muster. 'I'm pregnant!'

Dumfounded, her father rushed up with a chair. 'Here, sit down love. Take it easy.' He moistened his lips. 'Did you say... baby?'

The General, not to be outdone, offered another one, complete with cushion. 'That's no good, m'dear. Try this – much more comfortable.'

Len licked his lips. 'Don't worry, darling, you can tell your old dad all about it – whose um, baby is it?'

Kate looked up innocently. 'Why, William's, of course. Who else?'

'But I thought you two were... having um problems.'

Laughing with amusement at the very idea, his daughter rebuked him teasingly. 'Just a silly tiff, Daddy. I'd forgotten all about it long ago. Why, surely you realise that. You don't mind?'

'Mind?' He laughed, somewhat over heartedly. 'Of course not, splendid fellow. I've always liked the lad. One of the best, eh General?'

Clutching his head in disbelief, the General forced a genial smile. 'We *are* talking about William, my son, are we, just to get the record straight?'

'Of course,' replied Kate demurely. 'You don't think I'd be carrying on with anyone else called William, do you?'

'No, of course not, damn it. That makes all the difference. What a young...' he hastily dismissed the word 'rogue' and changed it to, 'rascal, to be sure.'

He straightened up and, slightly embarrassed, offered his hand to his former despised Commie friend.

'This calls for a celebration, what? Sorry about my sounding off just now. Spoke without thinking. Slip of the tongue, you know.'

'That's all right, old man. Don't give it another thought.'

In the midst of all the mutual congratulations, Aunt Emma called the meeting to order. 'I don't know whether it has escaped your notice, gentlemen, but have you remembered to spare a thought about the plight of poor William?'

Kate sprang up, distraught, forgetting all about her playacting role. 'Of course. Don't just stand there, why don't we *do* something. Algy,' she appealed, 'isn't there anything we can do? We don't even know where he *is* or who would *know*!'

'There's only one person who would know the answer to that,' snorted the General, 'Bugsby, that's who. Frobisher, where are you?'

'Yes, sir.'

'Get him on the line.'

'I did try earlier, sir, but he was tied up with a VIP party.'

'The flypast is over now – tell him it's urgent.'

'Yes, sir.'

Pacing up and down, the General whacked his leg

impatiently with his cane while he was waiting. Directly the call came through he wasted no time. 'Is that you, Bugsby, Rodders here. Oh, you've heard about that mad escapade of theirs, have you? You don't have the details? I can bring you up to date on that. My adjutant tells me that your man Malone is steamed up about his young lady friend who's got herself in some trouble or other. Yes, Lavinia, you know about her, do you? Apparently, the story goes that she was assaulted by some wretched Commie on a boat in the harbour over here and he's hell bent on revenge. How? Well, I'm told he's got hold of some explosives or other from his father's oil well and plans to drop it on this feller's boat in retaliation.

'I know, barmy's the word all right. Anything you can do about it? Try ordering him down or something? No, I haven't got a fix you can use. What happens if he doesn't answer. He's a bit of a rebel, is he? You'll send up an escort to make sure? Good man. Remind me to stand you a drink when it's sorted. Same to you, old man. Bye.'

He turned to the others. 'I've done all I can do. Now it's up to the others. Confound it, if only I could speak to William and find out what he's up to.'

16

HERO OF THE HOUR

Gazing out despondently over the landscape below, slipping by at what seemed like a terrifying speed and bringing the imminent threat of decision time ever closer, William wished he did as well. In the distance he noticed a thin, wispy layer of cloud drifting towards them and the sight of it gave him the glimmer of an idea. If only the cloud was thick enough to hide them from the ship. His fervent hopes were interrupted by Chuck pulling himself up awkwardly next to him.

'This is where I leave you.'

'Are you thinking of jumping out?' asked William in alarm.

'Ha-ha, funny. Look, I've put it on a steady course that should take us dead over target. You take over while I get back to the doorway. Directly you see the ship let me know and I'll do the rest.' He flexed his hands in anticipation with grim satisfaction. 'That'll teach the bastard.'

'You know what you are doing, Chuck?' he asked without hope, all pretence gone between them.

'Yeah. He's got it coming to him.'

'They're other people on board... you realise that.'

'Hell, you don't think I'm going for a direct hit, do you, man? I'm just going to drop it alongside. That should make him sit up.'

William thought of the havoc likely. 'Why not drop a note to give them warning?'

'Too late for that – trust me,' and grabbing hold of his stick, he slowly made his way back along the flight deck, dragging his leg behind him.

Left alone William peered up into the sky, hoping for more cloud cover.

As if in answer to his prayers, a stray wisp passed by in front of him, then another. A few moments later, a thicker strand rolled towards them just as the ship itself swung into view below them like a toy.

'Any joy yet?'

'No,' lied William, secretly shifting the controls slightly, hoping his actions would not be noticed.

'Hell, we should be there by now.' His headphone buzzed. 'Yes? Not now, we're busy. Oh, it's you, Chief. What, only a routine flight. He's what? As if I'd do anything like that.'

Encouraged by the background interruption, William banked the plane slightly away from the immediate target area and made for the nearest cloud formation like a homing bird.

'Come back now? But what for? Oh, all right, as soon as we've finished. What d'you mean, now this minute? Has everyone got the jitters? Oh, all right.' He glanced up as William gave the thumbs-up sign at the sight of a patch of clear water below, before the cloud closed in again. 'If you say so, sir. Right away. Say, what do I need an escort for?' He pulled his headphones off disgustedly. 'I don't know what's got into the old man, he thinks we need a couple of nannies.' He dragged the nearest box towards him. 'Sorry about that, the old man's got a bee in his bonnet. Dammit, is that a cloud? I can't see a darn thing – are you sure we're in position?'

'Couldn't be better,' called out William, feeling quite weak with relief, now that the danger was passed. 'Are you all right back there?' he asked, hearing a series of curses followed by a muffled thud.

'Ow! I tripped over the damn thing, pushing it out. Nearly there. I can just about shift the other one. There... that's the lot. Geez, can you hold the fort for a bit, I can hardly move.'

William gulped, taking in the nerve-racking sight of the instrument panel in front of him. 'I'll do my best. What do I do next?'

'Take it easy. Just pull the stick over to the left and bank slightly. That's it, carry on like that for a moment. Ouch, this blasted foot. I should have put it on auto pilot. Wait a minute, while I think.'

'But how do I get back?' asked William helplessly.

As if by magic, the clouds parted and two slim fighters appeared from nowhere, blocking their flight path. They closed in and took up position either side of the Dakota and waved at them to follow.

'There's your answer, Bill,' cried Chuck joyfully. 'I never thought I'd be so pleased to see the good old USA know-how turning up.' He lay back thankfully.

'Now, Bill, do exactly what they tell you and keep a good distance, so you don't run into anybody.'

'It's all very well for you, you're not in the hot seat. This isn't the trainer – everything's different.' Trying to remember all Chuck had taught him in the past few days, William hitched himself closer to the controls and concentrated on following the leaders, careful to keep a clear distance from the two escorts. After what seemed hours of unrelenting pressure, faithfully following on the path of the two leading aircraft ahead, William was just about reaching the limit of endurance when one of the planes dipped its wing and started losing height.

'Remember what I told you,' called out Chuck. 'Ease the stick back on the approach, not too fast now, gently does it.'

The Dakota steadied, touched down briefly then lifted off for a moment and came down again with a thump. Before he could do anything, the dashboard panel seemed to leap up at him and then all was darkness.

As he came to and began to focus gradually on his immediate surroundings all he could make out were a row of empty beds and the beaming face of a matron bending over him, whose face appeared vaguely familiar.

'How are we today?' she asked archly, twittering like a hen.

'Eh, what?' William shifted his position to avoid her looming presence.

'What does it feel like to be the hero of the hour?' she simpered, smoothing the sheet over him coyly.

'What are you talking about?'

'You do know that half of Fleet Street are waiting outside to hear about your fantastic exploits, and a top ranking American General who tells me he must see you right away before anyone?' She stood there almost purring with satisfaction, revelling at the unexpected publicity the hospital was receiving. 'And he's not the only one.' She gave a little wriggle of anticipation. 'There's the gentleman who was with you in the aircraft, and a young lady who says she's a friend of yours, and your family and dozens of people, all queuing up to see you.' Seeing his worried expression, she felt duty bound to ask. 'Are you up to receiving visitors?' Without waiting for an answer, aware of the overwhelming benefits to her hospital, she added brightly, 'The doctor says you may be still suffering from mild concussion, but as long as you don't overdo it, you should be fine.'

Thinking back about the recent shattering events, William

decided that he'd better see the American General first in case it meant cooking up a story to save his friend Chuck. 'Did he say his name?'

'Yes, indeed.' She consulted her notes and told him reverently, 'A Major General McKinrick.'

William hitched himself up, fearing the worst. 'You'd better show him in.'

Before he had a chance to finish his sentence, the door was pushed open and the burly shape of his father's old friend bounded in.

'Bill, I hope you don't mind me busting in like this, old son, but I had to see you.'

'Pull up a chair, sir, I needed to see you anyway.' William started explaining.

Waving the preliminaries aside, his visitor launched into his own news.

'I've heard all about your great efforts to save old Chuck from making a complete idiot of himself and I'm immensely grateful, I'm telling you.'

'It was nothing, sir,' insisted William loyally.

'Don't give me that whitewash, I can't believe he acted the way he did and on top of that, landing you in it as well.'

'He's always been very good to me.'

'And where would he have been without you, I ask myself. Never mind that. You'll be pleased to know that you managed to land that old Dak of ours without hardly a scratch on her.'

'I'm so glad.'

'And because of your prompt action at the eleventh hour, that little,' he glanced around cautiously, '*present* he was delivering missed his target by a mile, so no harm was done. As for that idiot, he frankly deserves a court martial but if you're willing to overlook his actions.'

'Oh, certainly. He is a bit of an ass, but he was egged onto it by that girlfriend of his.'

'Don't I know it,' he sighed. 'He's landed himself with a heap of problems there but he's old enough to work that out for himself. In that case,' he grinned broadly, 'you'll be pleased to know that he doesn't need our help any longer. He's decided to give up his commission on compassionate grounds. He doesn't need his Air Force pay any longer.'

'Oh, why's that?' William was intrigued.

'Didn't anyone tell you? His old man's struck lucky with that oil stake of his – he's got a gusher!'

'No!' William was delighted. 'He's been talking about it for days.'

His visitor got up briskly. 'I'll leave him to tell you all about it. He's waiting outside.' Bending over to shake hands he said, 'I think that action of yours has repaid the debt I owe him for saving my life that time. Look after yourself and remind me to your dad and tell him I'll be forever grateful to you for getting us out of that mess. Goodbye, son.'

After a few minutes, Chuck's head appeared around the door. 'Is he gone? Good.' The rest of him appeared, complete with crutches.

'Are you still suffering?'

'No, I don't really need these.' He threw the supports aside carelessly. 'It was the only way I could get past Matron, the old battle axe.' He held up a hand. 'Just called in to say thanks for everything before we're off.'

'Congrats and all that. I'm so pleased to hear about your good fortune.'

'Not half as much as I am.' He stuck his chest out proudly. 'Not only that. You'll never guess.' He waited expectantly and carried on, not waiting a second longer and burst out proudly. 'My gorgeous beloved has said "Yes" and here she is to tell you about it herself.'

The door opened and Lavinia appeared, closely followed by her mother, Mrs Muriel Fox Cuddles.

'My love, allow me to introduce you to my best friend who literally saved my life – William.'

After a pregnant pause, Lavinia took one look and drew herself up haughtily. 'I'm afraid we are not acquainted, are we Mumsie?'

Her mother narrowed her gaze, giving him a blank stare. 'Never seen him in my life, darling. How do you do.'

Before William could think of an adequate response, she gathered up her furs. 'Now, if we can tear you away, Chuck darling, we do have a train to catch.'

'Of course.' Chuck automatically turned to follow and called back rather apologetically, 'I'm sorry about the rush, Bill, but we are rather pushed for time. Glad you've at last met up. Bye, old man. I was hoping to get you to be best man, but Lavinia was keen to get to know my dad, now we're engaged. I'll keep in touch – thanks for everything.'

'Whew!' William sank back gratefully, feeling as if an enormous weight had been cast off for good. 'At least that's one problem solved.'

Then, to crown his happiness, the door flew open and Kate catapulted in, throwing herself at him and smothering him with kisses.

'Oh, my darling, you're safe. Thank heavens – will you ever forgive me?'

'Wh-at? Is it really you? I can't believe it.' He stroked the back of her head as he attempted to come to terms with what she was saying to him over and over again, between kisses.

'Oh, darling, when I think you nearly killed yourself trying to save that wretched Borshak, I nearly died!'

'William attempted to get the facts straight. 'Does that mean you still care for me after I behaved so badly?'

'Of course, I was only being silly. Will you forgive me?'

For an answer he drew her closer. 'Of course, my darling. Does that mean you'll marry me after all?'

She smiled impishly. 'You'll have to, now I'm having a baby, won't you?'

He caught his breath and repeated foolishly. 'Baby? Did you say - baby?'

She giggled. 'That was only to stop Daddy and your pa coming to blows. It was only pretend, and they believed me.'

'Whatever you've done seems to have done the trick,' he marvelled. 'Why didn't I think of a wheeze like that?'

'Because you're only a man.' She pulled his head down again. 'I don't care if they don't find that blessed treasure they keep talking about, as long as we're together.'

'Quite right,' he agreed contentedly.

'At least you stopped that man letting off those dreadful bombs, so nobody was hurt, thank goodness, so Daddy can go on looking for it, if he wants to. Although,' she murmured, 'it would have been nice to know it was there in case we were really stuck for cash. It's a good thing Aunt Emma came to the rescue in time.'

They were interrupted by a tap at the door.

'Oh, tush, not another visitor. I wonder who that could be?' She stretched herself reluctantly and sat up. 'Who's that?'

'Excuse me for butting in,' came the answer. To William's surprise it turned out to be his uncle, Lord Beddington.

'I say, I hope you don't mind, but seeing as you're only down the corridor.'

A light of understanding flashed in William's mind. 'Of course, this is your hospital, Uncle, I didn't realise. I wondered why Matron looked so familiar.'

His uncle coughed apologetically. 'I thought you might have heard the latest developments.'

'No, what's that?' William asked, still caught up in his happy state of euphoria.

'I don't suppose you would, stuck in here.' His uncle paused, working out the best way of breaking the glad tidings.

'I've just heard on the news. Those bombs you let off managed to dislodge an old shipwreck full of treasure and it's got washed up in my bay, so they're saying I'm entitled to claim ownership.' As the news sank in, he explained happily, 'According to some papers they've found, it was given to my jolly old ancestors by his Lordship for their sterling work in fighting the Spaniards and bringing back hoards of captured bounty.' He thought about it for a bit. 'I suppose that means I'm a rich man, funny that.'

'Why, that's marvellous!' exclaimed William. 'What are you going to do with it all?' he enthused, delighted at his uncle's unexpected good fortune. 'Now you'll be able to grow masses of new greengage trees,' he added mischievously, remembering his uncle's accident with the ladder.

His uncle reflected thoughtfully. 'Now that the Memsahib is better I suppose we can really get down to supporting St. Mary's again in its hour of need and putting your aunt back in charge of the Council, if she's still feeling up to it. Not only that,' his voice warmed, 'I've always been dashed proud of my old ancestors. As well as restoring the Hall to its former glories, I'm going to get in touch with your dad, Kate, and see it we can't put some fresh life into that marina scheme of his and make the port thrive again.'

His news was received with a squeal from Kate who bounded up and kissed him joyfully.

'Thanks, Uncle,' William added gratefully.

His uncle beamed with appreciation. 'If it hadn't been for you, my lad, I'd still be up to my ears in debt.' Coming to a decision, he informed the delighted couple, 'Just for that, I'm going to see your action does not go unrewarded.' He gazed at them fondly. 'As soon as get my hands on the money, I'm going to make you my heir and share half the proceeds with you. How about that for starters?'

Dear reader,

We hope you enjoyed reading *The Duncans Are Coming*. Please take a moment to leave a review, even if it's a short one. Your opinion is important to us.

Discover more books by Michael N. Wilton at

https://www.nextchapter.pub/authors/michael-n-wilton

Want to know when one of our books is free or discounted? Join the newsletter at

http://eepurl.com/bqqB3H

Best regards,

Michael N. Wilton and the Next Chapter team

You could also like:
Don't Bank On It Sweetheart by Michael N. Wilton

To read the first chapter for free, please head to:
https://www.nextchapter.pub/books/dont-bank-on-it-
sweetheart

ABOUT THE AUTHOR

Following National Service in the RAF Michael returned to banking, until an opportunity arose to pursue a career in writing. After working as a press officer for several electrical engineering companies, he was asked to set up a central press office as a group press officer for an engineering company. From there he moved on to become publicity manager for a fixed wing and helicopter charter company, where he was involved in making a film of the company's activities at home and overseas.

He became so interested in filming that he joined up with a partner to make industrial films for several years, before ending his career handling research publicity for a national gas transmission company.

Since retiring he has fulfilled his dream of becoming a writer and has written two books for children as well as several romantic comedies.

You can read more about Michael on his website:
www.michaelwilton.co.uk
Amazon:
https://www.amazon.co.uk/Michael-N.-Wilton/e/B00EPG3SF4

BOOKS BY MICHAEL N. WILTON

Save Our Shop

Introducing William Bridge

Losing his job at the local newspaper after depicting the sub-editor in a series of unflattering doodles, William Bridge is called on to help his uncle Albert keep his shop going. The first thing he does is fall in love with Sally, the latest shop volunteer, despite formidable opposition from her autocratic stepmother, Lady Courtney.

Following a break-in and lost orders, an SOS sent to Albert's maverick brother Neil for back-up support changes everything. On the run from the police, Neil disguises himself and encourages William to be nice to a visiting American security expert and his flighty daughter Veronica to promote business, causing a rift in the budding romance.

The pressure mounts for William to investigate rumours of a shady deal to take over the shop and threaten the life of the village. William is willing to pay almost any price in his desperate fight to win back his love and save the shop.

Amazon: My Book

Amazon UK: My Book

In The Soup

Once again, William Bridge must put aside his ambitions to become a writer and marry his sweetheart Sally when her father, Sir Henry, is involved in a scandal that threatens to put an end to the family's hopes of getting their son Lancelot married to the daughter of a wealthy American security expert.

Foiled in his attempts to get his own back, Foxey Fred and his gang find a new way of retrieving their fortunes by blackmailing Sir Henry who, fearful his wife may find out, appeals to William for help. Calling on his Uncle Neil for support, William sets out to unravel the threads of lies and deceit despite continued opposition from Sally's stepmother, Lady Courtney, and a series of female encounters that are enough to test the trust of even the most faithful admirers.

Amazon.com: My Book

Amazon UK: My Book

The Spy Who Couldn't Count

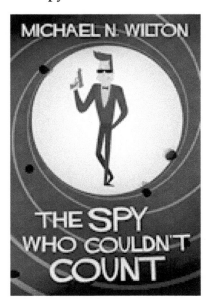

Inflicting Christian names like Jefferson Youll on a young lad already saddled with a surname like Patbottom is a sufficient handicap for anyone, but if you have the misfortune to be educated at somewhere like Watlington County Grammar and end up as thick as a plank and can't even count, life gets very tricky indeed. Settling for Jyp and braving a succession of dead end jobs, he finds sanctuary in a Government statistics department dealing with figures, much to the hilarity of his father.

To escape the amorous attention of his ever helpful colleague, Jyp panics and dives into another office where he is recruited by one of Britain's security departments after a hilarious interview in which he is mistaken for a trained spy killer.

Despite his initial bumbling efforts, he takes on a fight to unmask a series of trusted spies in the heart of Whitehall in a desperate battle to win the hand of his true love.

Amazon.com: My Book

Amazon UK: My Book

~

Don't Bank On It Sweetheart

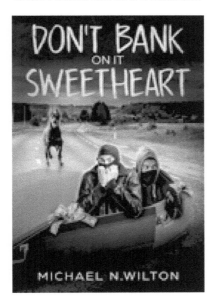

To aspiring writer Arthur Conway, the job offer from a small bank proves a welcome haven - especially with his mounting bills.

But Alastair - his cousin who works at the same bank - sees Arthur's arrival as an opportunity to unlock the fortunes of the bank while the manager is away. When his scheme fails, a new manager takes over with a bold plan to transform the bank.

After Arthur falls in love with Jenny, the young consultant brought in, he faces stiff competition from her pet dog Ben.

Spurned by his love in a jealous misunderstanding, can Arthur foil an attempt to rob the bank and win her love?

Amazon.com: My Book

Amazon UK: My Book

CHILDREN'S BOOKS

Grandad Bracey and the Flight to Seven Seas

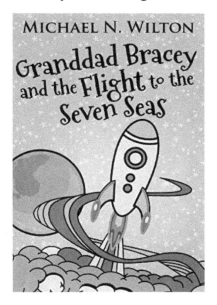

When retired captain James Clipper gets his nickname, Granddad Bracey, he little realizes that it will involve them in an epic adventure on a far-away planet called Seven Seas.

There, together with his granddaughter Sally, they have to battle against all odds to save her mother's life.

Amazon.com: My Book

Amazon.uk: My Book

Happenings at Hookwood

When a trusting young rabbit called Startup sets out to help his wildlife friends, he little expects to find himself being enticed by a slinky-looking rabbit called Lola. They end up in a life-or-death struggle to stop King Freddie, and a horde of brown rats, from taking over their beloved Hookwood.

Amazon.com: My Book

Amazon.uk: My Book

The Duncans Are Coming
ISBN: 978-4-86751-366-8

Published by
Next Chapter
1-60-20 Minami-Otsuka
170-0005 Toshima-Ku, Tokyo
+818035793528

1st July 2021

Lightning Source UK Ltd.
Milton Keynes UK
UKHW010920250721
387681UK00001B/116

9 784867 513668